T H E

G I R L

H E

W I S H E D

(A Paige King Mystery—Book Four)

BLAKE PIERCE

Blake Pierce

Blake Pierce is the USA Today bestselling author of the RILEY PAGE mystery series, which includes seventeen books. Blake Pierce is also the author of the MACKENZIE WHITE mystery series, comprising fourteen books; of the AVERY BLACK mystery series, comprising six books; of the KERI LOCKE mystery series, comprising five books; of the MAKING OF RILEY PAIGE mystery series, comprising six books; of the KATE WISE mystery series, comprising seven books; of the CHLOE FINE psychological suspense mystery, comprising six books; of the JESSE HUNT psychological suspense thriller series, comprising twenty-four books; of the AU PAIR psychological suspense thriller series, comprising three books; of the ZOE PRIME mystery series, comprising six books; of the ADELE SHARP mystery series, comprising sixteen books, of the EUROPEAN VOYAGE cozy mystery series, comprising four books; of the new LAURA FROST FBI suspense thriller, comprising nine books (and counting); of the new ELLA DARK FBI suspense thriller, comprising eleven books (and counting); of the A YEAR IN EUROPE cozy mystery series, comprising nine books, of the AVA GOLD mystery series, comprising six books (and counting); of the RACHEL GIFT mystery series, comprising six books (and counting); of the VALERIE LAW mystery series, comprising nine books (and counting); of the PAIGE KING mystery series, comprising six books (and counting); of the MAY MOORE mystery series, comprising nine books (and counting); of the CORA SHIELDS mystery series, comprising three books (and counting); and of the NICKY LYONS mystery series, comprising three books (and counting).

An avid reader and lifelong fan of the mystery and thriller genres, Blake loves to hear from you, so please feel free to visit www.blakepierceauthor.com to learn more and stay in touch.

BOOKS BY BLAKE PIERCE

NICKY LYONS MYSTERY SERIES
ALL MINE (Book #1)
ALL HIS (Book #2)
ALL HE SEES (Book #3)

CORA SHIELDS MYSTERY SERIES
UNDONE (Book #1)
UNWANTED (Book #2)
UNHINGED (Book #3)

MAY MOORE SUSPENSE THRILLER
NEVER RUN (Book #1)
NEVER TELL (Book #2)
NEVER LIVE (Book #3)
NEVER HIDE (Book #4)
NEVER FORGIVE (Book #5)
NEVER AGAIN (Book #6)
NEVER LOOK BACK (Book #7)
NEVER FORGET (Book #8)
NEVER LET GO (Book #9)

PAIGE KING MYSTERY SERIES
THE GIRL HE PINED (Book #1)
THE GIRL HE CHOSE (Book #2)
THE GIRL HE TOOK (Book #3)
THE GIRL HE WISHED (Book #4)
THE GIRL HE CROWNED (Book #5)
THE GIRL HE WATCHED (Book #6)

VALERIE LAW MYSTERY SERIES
NO MERCY (Book #1)
NO PITY (Book #2)
NO FEAR (Book #3)
NO SLEEP (Book #4)
NO QUARTER (Book #5)
NO CHANCE (Book #6)

NO REFUGE (Book #7)
NO GRACE (Book #8)
NO ESCAPE (Book #9)

RACHEL GIFT MYSTERY SERIES
HER LAST WISH (Book #1)
HER LAST CHANCE (Book #2)
HER LAST HOPE (Book #3)
HER LAST FEAR (Book #4)
HER LAST CHOICE (Book #5)
HER LAST BREATH (Book #6)
HER LAST MISTAKE (Book #7)
HER LAST DESIRE (Book #8)

AVA GOLD MYSTERY SERIES
CITY OF PREY (Book #1)
CITY OF FEAR (Book #2)
CITY OF BONES (Book #3)
CITY OF GHOSTS (Book #4)
CITY OF DEATH (Book #5)
CITY OF VICE (Book #6)

A YEAR IN EUROPE
A MURDER IN PARIS (Book #1)
DEATH IN FLORENCE (Book #2)
VENGEANCE IN VIENNA (Book #3)
A FATALITY IN SPAIN (Book #4)

ELLA DARK FBI SUSPENSE THRILLER
GIRL, ALONE (Book #1)
GIRL, TAKEN (Book #2)
GIRL, HUNTED (Book #3)
GIRL, SILENCED (Book #4)
GIRL, VANISHED (Book 5)
GIRL ERASED (Book #6)
GIRL, FORSAKEN (Book #7)
GIRL, TRAPPED (Book #8)
GIRL, EXPENDABLE (Book #9)
GIRL, ESCAPED (Book #10)
GIRL, HIS (Book #11)

LAURA FROST FBI SUSPENSE THRILLER
ALREADY GONE (Book #1)
ALREADY SEEN (Book #2)
ALREADY TRAPPED (Book #3)
ALREADY MISSING (Book #4)
ALREADY DEAD (Book #5)
ALREADY TAKEN (Book #6)
ALREADY CHOSEN (Book #7)
ALREADY LOST (Book #8)
ALREADY HIS (Book #9)

EUROPEAN VOYAGE COZY MYSTERY SERIES
MURDER (AND BAKLAVA) (Book #1)
DEATH (AND APPLE STRUDEL) (Book #2)
CRIME (AND LAGER) (Book #3)
MISFORTUNE (AND GOUDA) (Book #4)
CALAMITY (AND A DANISH) (Book #5)
MAYHEM (AND HERRING) (Book #6)

ADELE SHARP MYSTERY SERIES
LEFT TO DIE (Book #1)
LEFT TO RUN (Book #2)
LEFT TO HIDE (Book #3)
LEFT TO KILL (Book #4)
LEFT TO MURDER (Book #5)
LEFT TO ENVY (Book #6)
LEFT TO LAPSE (Book #7)
LEFT TO VANISH (Book #8)
LEFT TO HUNT (Book #9)
LEFT TO FEAR (Book #10)
LEFT TO PREY (Book #11)
LEFT TO LURE (Book #12)
LEFT TO CRAVE (Book #13)
LEFT TO LOATHE (Book #14)
LEFT TO HARM (Book #15)

THE AU PAIR SERIES
ALMOST GONE (Book#1)
ALMOST LOST (Book #2)
ALMOST DEAD (Book #3)

CHAPTER ONE

Meredith Park couldn't shake the feeling that she was being watched, as she slowly started to get ready to leave the restaurant at the Lexington Ren-Faire.

Which was silly, because of *course* she was being watched. Being watched was a large part of her job, there at the Ren-Faire. Even if she was actually just there to serve food and make sure that the kitchens didn't overcook the roast suckling pig, she knew that she was as much a part of the act of the place as any of the performers there. Just looking around now, there were at least a dozen people watching her performance.

"I hope your meal was ok," Meredith said, offering a smile to a young couple who had come in wearing their own interpretations of medieval dress, both of them wearing chainmail that looked like they'd put it together at home from loops of plastic and then spray painted it. She set the bill down for them and made her way around to the next table, gently working her way towards the exit. Meredith wouldn't be able to leave until she'd cleared the last tables, checked her share of the tips, and made sure that the others were ok before she headed home.

It wasn't easy, being a wench. That was Meredith Park's official job title: serving wench at the court of King Arthur. Because apparently the people who ran the Lexington Ren-Faire thought that was the most period appropriate way to describe their staff members. Meredith wasn't entirely sure that it was the job title she would have chosen for herself if they'd asked, but they hadn't.

At the same time, though, Meredith had to admit that she loved working there in the restaurant of the Ren-Faire. She loved the enjoyment that people got from visiting, and she loved the enthusiasm that some of them showed. The cosplayers always loved to get involved, piecing together chainmail at home and sewing dresses that made the ones Meredith had to wear for work look drab by comparison. Some days, it was hard to tell the visitors from the people who worked there, although it helped that Meredith knew everyone who worked there. They all passed through the restaurant sooner or later.

1

Meredith bussed the last of the tables in her section, then handed over to the next wench on duty. She smiled and waved as she left the restaurant, in one last piece of performance. She always went home in her work clothes because no one there wanted to see the medieval servant who had just been providing their food come out in jeans and a t-shirt.

Meredith had majored in history at college, so taking a job at the local Renaissance Faire while she tried to work out what else she wanted to do with her life had seemed like a great option. And it was, just as long as Meredith didn't pay too much attention to the portrayals of history on display there and just went along with the fun of the place.

For a start, King Arthur? If the mythical king had existed at all, he'd probably been an early medieval king in one of the small British kingdoms of the time; he had probably lived close to a thousand years before the Renaissance.

Then there was the wench's costume that Meredith had been given for work. It had a great flounced skirt, a bonnet, and a corset that was more of a bustier, over a pale linen underskirt. By actual medieval standards, Meredith suspected that she was several layers of clothing short of authenticity; but at the Ren-Faire, showing off how one looked apparently counted for far more. It was about how impressed the patrons were, not whether everything fit with the latest historical papers.

Not that Meredith minded a little showing off, or the attention that got her here. She was five-ten, full-figured and blonde-haired, with deep blue eyes that were a little larger and more wide-set than most people's. With her slightly rounded features and ready smile, it had been pretty much inevitable that she would end up as a wench.

Meredith had been briefly annoyed by that because a part of her would rather have been a knight, but there was a waiting list to become a knight, or a jester, or any of the entertainment jobs. Meredith had quickly found that she had a knack for cooking good food, and for serving customers. She'd even done extra research on medieval recipes, trying to find ones that would fit with modern tastes while still seeming authentic enough.

Meredith had quickly found herself in charge of a whole section in the restaurant, in what would have been a promotion to manager anywhere else. Here, of course, she was just called "chief restaurant wench," but it was ok. The money was good, and the people she worked with were great. Ok, so they were occasionally a little strange, but wasn't everyone?

Meredith headed out into the fair, taking in the early evening air. There were still plenty of people around, moving between tents and booths, old fashioned steam rides that were still about five hundred years too recent, and staff members who wandered the crowds juggling or tumbling, making fun of people for their strange modern dress or selling them snacks out of barrows.

Meredith had to admit that, in spite of the anachronisms, she loved it here. There was nowhere else she would rather work. Historical authenticity didn't matter once you understood the joy a place like this brought to people when they visited. They came here and they went away smiling, pretty much regardless of who they were. There weren't many jobs where Meredith could say that about the people she met.

She headed for the employee parking lot, taking off her bonnet as she went. It was still hard to shake the feeling of being stared at, but as Meredith glanced around, she couldn't see anyone who was actually looking her way now. At least not any more than usual. She was just one more person moving through the crowds of the Ren-Faire. No one seemed to be giving her particular attention.

Meredith shrugged and kept going. If someone was staring at her, giving her unwelcome attention, so what? The Ren-Faire attracted its share of creeps as well as those people just there to enjoy themselves. There were always a few guys who just wanted to stare at women in old fashioned dresses, or who crowded around whenever one volunteered to be put in the stocks they kept in the main square. Guys who longed for things to be the way they'd been in some version of the past that only really existed in their own heads.

Meredith had learned to just ignore that side of things. The good definitely outweighed the bad, after all. She needed to get home, so she hurried on towards the parking lot. Her small Citroen was waiting there, sitting underneath the shade of a large beech tree to keep it cool. Meredith fished her keys out of the pouch on her belt that she had in place of a purse, meaning that she could keep things with her without having to break out of the dress code for the Ren-Faire.

Slowly, Meredith started to slide out of what she thought of as her medieval mode, starting to think about her much more modern life again. When she got home, she would get changed, maybe call a couple of her friends, see if they wanted to go out…

"Meredith!"

Hearing her name called was enough to make Meredith stop and turn, wondering if it was one of the other employees of the Renaissance Faire. Maybe something had happened with the restaurant, or they wanted someone to fill in for an hour. Meredith could definitely use the overtime.

It wasn't an employee, though, or at least, Meredith didn't think he was. It was hard to tell, given the strange way the man was dressed, but she didn't recognize him, and Meredith thought that she knew everyone who worked there.

He was advancing on her slowly, a look of cold menace transfixing Meredith as he did so.

"You have transgressed," he said. "You have ignored the order of things, the sumptuary laws, spoken seditiously to your king…"

"I don't know what this is," Meredith said. "Is this some performance piece for the Ren-Faire? Because I'm going home."

She started to back away towards her car.

That was when she saw the knife in his hand. Meredith panicked then, turning, and running for her car.

Her feet tangled in her dress as she did so, sending Meredith tumbling to the ground. Her keys spilled from her hand, spinning away from her.

"Trying to take to your carriage, you villain? Ahead of your betters? The order of precedence demands satisfaction!"

Meredith was on her back now, staring up at him, at the knife that seemed so strange and so deadly. She opened her mouth to scream for help…

That was when he leapt at her.

CHAPTER TWO

Agent Paige King of the FBI was trying to build a profile for a killer. She was piecing information together, drawing out every psychological and evidential scrap, trying to glean every hint she could and work out what it meant, fitting it together in new combinations to try to establish anything she could about the man she was hunting.

She *would* find enough pieces of the puzzle to catch the Exsanguination Killer. She had to do it, for her father, and for the damage that had been done to Paige's life since his death. Maybe if she found the killer, the nightmares of standing over her father, of being the one to find him, would finally start to fade away.

Currently, Paige was building the profile while sitting on the couch in her apartment, her notes spread out around her. Ordinarily, her apartment was small and neat, because Paige liked to keep things perfectly in order, perfectly under her control. Now, though, the scattering of papers made the whole place seem cluttered, so that it was hard to tell where anything was beneath the wash of them.

She had her laptop open, with her files on the Exsanguination Killer pulled up, along with the latest news reports on the most recent murder. Paige was trying to find anything in them that was new, anything that she hadn't heard before.

Paige knew how she must look, sitting cross legged at the heart of it all, her slightly built frame hunched in like the focal point for some bizarre, paper based art installation designed to illustrate chaos at work. Her red hair was tangled from where Paige's fingers had twined in it whenever she'd felt frustration, and that had been often enough that she knew it must look like some kind of strange bird's nest arrangement now. Her green eyes were slightly bloodshot from having worked on this too long without a break.

She would take that break when she'd finally found something. When she'd worked out where the new information she'd obtained fit into the broader pattern of it all and she actually managed to find the killer.

Paige had gotten that information from Agent Sauer, her new boss at the FBI, after she'd solved her first case as an agent. She'd been able to see the files on the case, looking them over and trying to memorize as much as she could because Paige had known even then that there was no way she was going to get to take it out of Quantico to look through at her leisure.

Paige had at least some of what she needed, though. She knew now that there were facets to this that didn't come through in the news, facets that hadn't been released to the public by the FBI. That gave Paige some hope that there might be a chance to capture the killer, that the avenues she'd already exhausted weren't the only ways to get closer to the Exsanguination Killer.

She'd already known about the killer's methods: that they targeted both men and women, seemingly without a victim profile, drugging and then restraining them before opening their veins and letting them bleed out slowly. Paige knew that part better than anyone.

She'd seen what had happened to her father. She'd been fourteen when she'd been the one to find his body out in the woods, and even now, the horror of that moment sat in Paige's chest. If she closed her eyes now, she was back there, staring down at him, seeing the darkened soil around him where the blood had run into it, the horrifying pallor of his body, robbed of his life blood by the wounds the killer had inflicted.

Paige shook her head, trying to focus. She needed to think clearly.

She'd learned other parts of the killer's methods in the years since her father's murder: that the killer struck in sets of three, and so far had killed more than twenty people that they knew about. That he always struck in outdoor areas to allow evidence to be washed away, or disturbed by animals to the point where it wasn't usable.

But there had been two new things in the files that her boss had let Paige see, two new facets that might or might not reshape the spread of the papers and notes around Paige into some new arrangement. The first was a clue about the murder weapon: something small and extremely sharp, like a scalpel. That word brought all kinds of possibilities to Paige's mind. Was this someone with medical training? Was this about the killer valuing precision, or maybe even disliking the idea of causing excessive physical damage as they killed?

Was this something that seemed impossible: a squeamish serial killer?

No, Paige didn't believe that. Especially not given the second piece of evidence that Agent Sauer had dropped into her lap. The killer had left notes at the first kills of each cycle of three, taunting the police and telling them that they couldn't catch him. Those notes were short and to the point, but they weren't the sign of someone who shied away from what they did.

Instead, the taunting in them suggested a killer who was focused on the power the act of killing provided over others, and who liked the control they had over their victims. They killed neatly, not out of any horror about the blood, but to prove that they had so much control over the situation that they could do it that way. Killing slowly, killing precisely, was just another way of proving their power.

Paige was certain that they watched while their victims died. Why else kill using such a slow method? It wasn't about causing more pain, because the method chosen didn't involve torture or pain, but it *did* involve a victim who was conscious, slowly feeling their life blood ebbing from them. Everything about the killer's MO said that the kill wasn't the whole thing for them; it was about sitting back and watching the impact that it caused.

It was the beginnings of a profile, suggesting things about the killer that might lead to more, given time. The only problem was that just knowing that didn't help Paige get closer to who had done this. Maybe the FBI would be able to do something with the letter, but they'd had those before and hadn't found anything. In the absence of anything else, it wasn't enough to go on.

The frustration of that made Paige push her notes to one side. Even as she did so, her phone went off. Agent Sauer's name came up on the screen, and Paige answered her boss's call instantly.

"Agent King," he said, in his usual clipped, gruff tone, all business. "How soon can you get into Quantico?"

"Less than an hour, sir," Paige said. If she drove hard, she could do it.

"*Make* it less," Sauer said.

"Why? What's going on?"

"There's another killer for you and Agent Marriott to chase, and I need you on the case right away."

*

Paige drove into Quantico as fast as she dared, wondering what had Agent Sauer calling her in so urgently. He'd said that there was a killer, but for him to insist that she get over there as quickly as possible, it had to be a bad one.

As she arrived, she hurried to the third floor of the building that housed the BAU behind ivy covered walls, pausing only long enough to go through the obligatory security checks at the door. Even with her ID as a federal agent, she still had to pass through layers of scanners before she could even get into the building. It was just another reminder of the importance, and potential danger, of the job that she did now.

Sauer was waiting for her in a glass walled conference room on the third floor. He was a knife-thin man in his forties, with thin features and a dark beard. He wasn't the only one in there. Agent Christopher Marriott was there already, tall and broad shouldered, with sandy hair and boyish good looks. He was wearing a regulation dark suit that fit him well, and stood at one side of the room expectantly as if he'd been waiting for Paige to arrive for a while now.

Paige felt the same flare of attraction that she always felt when she saw him, because almost from the first moment she'd met Christopher, she'd felt a kind of connection to him that had been hard to explain, but that had drawn her towards him. That attraction was quickly followed by a now familiar sense of guilt. Christopher was a married man, and her partner in the FBI. Not only could nothing happen between them, just thinking about it felt wrong. Sometimes, in spite of how well they worked together, it made just being near him difficult.

"Paige, how are you?" Christopher asked. "Are you ok?"

There was a faint note of worry in his voice, and Paige realized that while she'd thrown on her own standard, cheap dark suit, she'd forgotten to untangle the mess of her hair. Christopher had obviously picked up on that small difference, and if Sauer had told him about the information he'd passed to her, maybe he understood some of her potential sources of worry. He would know that she'd been spending her time looking into her father's killer, and how that might affect her.

"I'm fine," Paige assured him. It didn't matter that it wasn't true. All that mattered was that she was there to do her job.

She looked over to Sauer with a hint of hope. He'd said that there'd been another death. Was it possible that this was about the one killer who had a connection to Paige? Was that why he'd called her in so quickly?

"Is this about the Exsanguination Killer?"

Paige had to ask it, had to hope that this was finally her chance to go after her father's killer. Even as she asked it, though, Agent Sauer was already shaking his head.

"I've told you before, we already have good agents working that case," he said. It was clear that it was an issue he wasn't about to give any ground on. He wasn't about to let her on the case in a hurry.

Was Paige really meant to stand back and not argue about that? Was she really just meant to accept that she couldn't be a part of the one investigation that had been the whole reason she had wanted to join the BAU in the first place?

She didn't have any choice, though, when it came to which cases she worked. She was an FBI agent now, and agents followed orders. There were other killers in the world beyond the Exsanguination Killer, killers she could help to put behind bars to stop them from ever hurting anyone else, and to bring some kind of closure to the families of the victims. That mattered too.

Paige saw Christopher look over with another expression of concern, obviously knowing how much the Exsanguination Killer case meant to Paige.

"If that case *does* need any extra agents at any point, sir..." he began, obviously understanding how much it meant to Paige, and trying to increase the chances of her getting to work on it.

"That's not the case I came here to talk to the two of you about," Sauer said, slightly more firmly. He gestured for the two of them to take a seat at a wide conference table. "We don't have a lot of time. This is a killer who seems to be killing at short intervals, and there's already a media storm over it."

Paige was at least able to control her feelings enough to be able to bring herself to sit next to Christopher. She understood now that a lot of the extremes of what she'd felt recently had been about the sudden reappearance of her father's killer. She could control herself, and sitting further away would only make things seem weird. It would increase the strangeness brought about by the attraction between them, not reduce it.

Sauer took out an iPad and called up images on it for the two of them to look at, obviously wanting them to see the situation before he started to explain it. The first photograph he showed them was a crime scene photograph of a young, blonde-haired woman lying on her back in a parking lot, her otherwise pale white dress stained red by blood. Paige winced at the sight of her there like that, even though she'd been expecting something like it. Even though she had seen plenty of bodies by now, it didn't get any easier. There was still the sense of pent up horror under the surface that always came to Paige when she saw the dead, but also a sense of anger, a need to correct the sudden wrongness in the world brought about by the killer.

Paige didn't know if she was transferring those feelings from what she felt about the Exsanguination Killer, or if it was just her natural reaction to the sight of the dead woman. It didn't matter. Either way, she knew as soon as she saw the body that she had to find answers.

"This is Meredith Park," Agent Sauer said. "Twenty-three years old. Until last night, she worked in the restaurant of the Lexington Kentucky Renaissance Faire. She was found dead by her colleagues in the employee parking lot. She'd been stabbed once, directly through the heart."

That was a tragedy, but there had to be more to this, or the local police department would be handling it. A single murder wasn't enough to bring in the FBI. It certainly wasn't enough to bring in a specialist unit dedicated to hunting serial killers.

"What's the serial killer angle, sir?" Christopher asked, obviously thinking the same thing that Paige was.

Sauer changed the picture on the iPad, showing a dark haired woman, probably in her thirties, lying propped against the wheel of a car. She was wearing a dark gray pantsuit, rather than the old fashioned style of dress Meredith had been wearing, but it was just as stained with blood. It was hard to believe that much blood could have come from inside one person, but Paige knew firsthand the reality of that.

"*This* is Gisele Newbury, thirty-five years old, a realtor. She was found dead outside her house by one of her neighbors two days ago, killed at around 5pm. Again, she died from a single stab wound to the heart."

That was an interesting similarity, but Paige still wasn't sure that it was enough.

"So what makes us think that the two are connected?" Paige asked. "Yes, the MO is similar, but stabbing is pretty common. The two cases don't have to be related."

"Because the killer left the same symbol behind at each scene," Sauer said, flicking over to the next image. It showed a small metal fleur-de-lis design, left there as if to lay claim to the murders.

"A calling card?" Christopher said. Paige saw him look her way. "How often does that happen?"

It was gratifying that Christopher looked to her expertise on these things, that he saw her as the expert on serial killers despite all the ones he'd helped to catch, but it also put pressure on Paige to be right.

"Not as often as people think," Paige replied. "The truth is that most serial killers just kill and move on. They don't work the way people think. They aren't this... *elaborate*."

They didn't need to be. A killer who *was* doing this was interesting. The fact that they were doing it said that there was something different about their pathology, something that it might be possible to latch on to.

Maybe that design would be enough to lead to him. Maybe it would point to a link between the victims that had gotten them both killed. Or maybe not. Maybe it was just a design that he liked and had decided to use. She and Christopher would only really find that out once they got to Kentucky. For now, what mattered was getting there. There was a killer out there, and if he'd killed two women in two days, then there was a sense of urgency to it. They needed to get out there before he had a chance to kill age. At least with *this* one, Paige had a chance to stop him before he managed to hurt anyone else.

CHAPTER THREE

Paige used the flight to Lexington to go over the case files for the murders on her computer and start doing some research. The more information she could get at this stage, the easier it would be to make connections once they got on the ground. She could feel the pressure of needing to be on top of it all, but Paige didn't let that slow her down.

As usual, the crime scene reports, coroner's reports, and everything the FBI's techs had been able to scrape from the victims' social media had all been uploaded to the FBI's systems for Paige to access. It meant a lot of information, but more information was better because there was a chance of finding a way through to the truth of all of this.

Christopher sat next to her on the flight, looking more relaxed than Paige felt. He'd looked through the files back in the meeting with Agent Sauer, but now seemed to be just waiting for their arrival in Kentucky before he did anything else.

"Why aren't you going over the files too?" Paige asked. She didn't mean it as if he wasn't pulling his weight. She just wanted to understand his working methods.

"I have the basics," Christopher said. "I want to see the situation on the ground before I make any decisions about it. Maybe you should too, Paige. You don't have to be the one doing all the work."

He seemed to be a man who liked to deal with the things in front of him, rather than speculating. He wanted to get answers through hard work and talking to people, rather than by theorizing based on the files. In a way, Paige liked that about him. That very down to earth approach made him a rock she could depend on as a partner, knowing that he was able to deal with whatever came at the two of them as a result of their cases.

At the same time, though, it meant that she was the one now who had to go through the files in detail, trying to find anything that might give them a head start on the case. She was the one who had to take the research side of things.

"Are you all right, Paige?" Christopher asked.

Paige thought for a moment that some of that dissatisfaction might have shown on her face, and she looked over to him with surprise that he'd managed to pick up on it so easily.

"Yes, why?"

"I mean, with the whole thing of the Exsanguination Killer being back. I know you were hoping Sauer was going to assign us to that. I know you'd rather work that case than this one."

That was true, as far as it went. Paige wanted to be there to make sure that the man who had killed her father finally faced justice. She wanted to be a part of *bringing* him to justice. Paige had put a lot into trying to find him so far, and just hearing that there was another murder attributed to him unsettled her. It was a part of why she was throwing herself into the research for this now. It at least helped to bury some of what she felt.

"It's… a difficult situation," Paige said. "My father meant everything to me. Being the one to find him dead changed something in me. It hurt more than anything else since. It tore my life and my mother's life apart. Without that one moment, we never would have ended up living with Jeremy…"

Jeremy, her stepfather. The one who had abused her until her mother had found out and taken them both out of the house right away. That hadn't taken away anything he'd done, though. He was in her nightmares as often as the Exsanguination Killer.

Christopher reached out as if he might put a comforting hand on her arm, because he knew all about Jeremy. Paige had told him. The two of them had even been to visit him, to warn him that an escaped killer might be about to target him. Paige hadn't been able to keep herself from punching Jeremy. Christopher had been there for her then, too.

Christopher pulled back, though. Maybe before Vegas, where they'd come so close to crossing the line with one another, he wouldn't have hesitated like that. But now, there seemed to be that wall of awkwardness between the two of them that neither one of them could breach. That it wouldn't be right to even try to breach. They both knew that they were attracted to one another, and they both knew that nothing could happen. Maybe they should have asked to be reassigned, but they worked too well together as partners for that.

"I feel like trying to do something to catch the man who did all that is the only way to make any of it better," Paige said. "If I catch him, maybe then some of the nightmares will stop."

Paige realized a second too late that she'd overstepped with that word. Of course, Christopher caught it.

"Nightmares?" Christopher asked. "I didn't know you had nightmares."

Paige knew that it was too late to deny it, so she nodded, instead. "Dr. Thornton calls it PTSD from everything that happened. I'll be there again, in the woods, just staring down at him..."

Paige shook her head. Her former Ph.D. supervisor's diagnosis notwithstanding, it wasn't something she was happy talking about now. It felt too personal, too intimate, and Christopher wasn't someone she could afford to get that close to. The more lines she crossed with him, the more chance there was of crossing one that she shouldn't.

"None of it matters," Paige said, even though that was a lie. It all mattered to her, more than she could express in words. It was there in the background every day of her life. "What matters now is that we catch *this* killer. He might only have two kills that we know about, but in a way, that's worrying."

"Why?" Christopher asked. Paige imagined that he could guess the answer to the question, but he obviously wanted to hear it from her. Maybe it was a way of passing the time on the flight, or maybe he just wanted to listen to her talk.

"Because it means we could be dealing with a spree killer," Paige said. "And that's far more dangerous."

"The distinction being..."

"Some serial killers operate over years," Paige explained. "They kill people at intervals, usually fairly regular intervals that mean something to them, or that represent how long they can go before the need to kill gets too great. Occasionally they pause when life events intervene, often they accelerate, but they never really stop. Spree killers... they still meet the definition of a serial killer because they kill multiple people in separate incidents, but they aren't lurking in the background unseen for months at a time. They try to kill as many people as they can in a short space of time."

"Meaning that this one will kill again and again over the next few days until he's caught?" Christopher said. Paige could hear the worry in his voice.

Paige nodded. That was the worst case scenario. Although there was one other possibility that was in some ways even worse.

"That's assuming that this is someone who has simply suffered a breakdown and decided to go on a killing spree," Paige said. "The

14

scarier possibility is that this is someone who has killed these victims for a reason, because once he achieves his aims, he might just disappear."

"And if he does that, then he might pop up later, killing again," Christopher said.

Paige nodded. Once someone had started trying to resolve their problems by killing people, it was easier for them to do it again. And if they were able to disappear, then they might never be found.

"What do you make of the elements Sauer brought up?" Christopher asked. "The unusual murder weapon and the symbol?"

"I'm looking through the coroner's report now," Paige said, pulling it up. It was hard to read the dry, almost cold way the coroner catalogued the women's injuries, noting defensive bruising to their arms that suggested their assailant had been in front of them when he attacked them. They'd seen the attack coming, tried to save their own lives, and been killed anyway. They hadn't been able to do anything to stop him.

"They have bruises that suggest they tried to fight back against their killer," Paige said, "but the only knife wounds are the single ones to the heart that killed them."

She saw Christopher frown at that. "Stabbings are usually messier, unless the killer takes their victim by surprise. Usually even then. Most people start stabbing, and they don't stop. And if someone fights back, their first instinct is to use the knife."

Which usually meant multiple cuts to the arms and body as the victim tried to prevent the knife from getting to them. But in this case, there hadn't been those wounds.

"So he was careful to only use the knife for the finish?" Paige said. "That sounds almost like ritual behavior, where he feels that he has to do things a particular way, either because it's what has worked for him in the past, or because it's the only way to guarantee the rush that comes from a kill."

Paige kept reading through the coroner's report, trying to glean anything else from what the coroner had said about the wounds. It was obviously something that meant a lot to the killer, otherwise why make such an effort to do things so precisely? Was there something in there that they could use to try to get closer to him?

Paige paused as she saw the coroner's notes on the likely murder weapon.

"There's something strange here too," Paige said. "The killer doesn't seem to have used a normal knife. The coroner says that it isn't like any knife he's seen."

"And he will have seen a lot of knife wounds," Christopher said. "Maybe if we get him to reconstruct the shape of the blade fully, it will tell us something."

"The preliminary report says that the wounds were square sided, more like the victims were stabbed with a sharpened fire poker than with a knife," Paige said. It was confusing because she'd never heard of a weapon like that. "Presumably that isn't what he used? People would notice someone carrying around a weapon like that."

Christopher shrugged. "At a Renaissance Faire? It's possible that people thought it was a part of a costume. But out on the street where Gisele Newbury was killed? I think that would stand out too much."

So it was probably something smaller, then. Something with a very unusual blade profile. Maybe, if they could identify exactly what it was, then it might help to move them closer to finding out who the killer was. Paige made a note of it as a possible line of inquiry.

For the moment, though, Paige had to keep looking for other possibilities.

"What do you make of the fleur-de-lis?" Paige asked Christopher. In some ways, it was the strangest part of all of this.

"It has to mean something to the killer, right?" Christopher said. "Why else go to the trouble of leaving it by both of the victims?"

"It's possible that it might be linked to the victims," Paige suggested. "It might be something relevant to both of them, rather than to him."

She started to look for any sign of that symbol in the social media profiles of the two women who had been killed. Maybe it might provide a link between the two of them and so point to some kind of reason why the two of them had been chosen as victims.

Paige couldn't find it anywhere, though. There wasn't *any* obvious connection between the two of them that she could find. There were no clear pictures of a design like that on the women's profiles, and a quick search for the design produced too many results to go through. The fleur-de-lis, meanwhile, was simply too much of a common design for it to be easy to find one person based on it. It cropped up in everything from fabrics to wallpaper, company logos to woodworking designs.

A little basic research suggested that it was a very old design. Paige found herself thinking about it in the context of the Renaissance Faire. Was the fleur-de-lis linked to that, or was it to do with something else?

"What I don't get is just how different the two victims appear to be," Paige said. "There's a restaurant worker in her early twenties, and a realtor in her mid-thirties. One was killed at a Renaissance Faire, the other outside her home. They don't look alike, they don't appear to have known one another, and I can't think of any obvious reason why the two of them might have been targeted. There has to be some kind of link, though."

Christopher shrugged. "If it's there, I'm sure you'll find it. The question now is what we should do once we're on the ground in Lexington. Do we try looking at Gisele Newbury or Meredith Park first? We'll need to look into both murders, but maybe if we get enough from one crime scene, it will give us a head start on the investigation."

Paige could understand that. The question was, with two such different murder victims, which one fit the killer better? Which one was closer to the killer's normal life? The temptation was to say the murder that *looked* more normal, out on the street, but Paige found herself thinking about the fleur-de-lis and the strange weapon.

That combination was enough to point Paige in the other direction.

"The two clues that we have so far have this vaguely medieval tinge to them," Paige said. "A strange dagger and an unusual symbol? Plus, Meredith Park is the most recent victim, so there's more of a chance of finding something that isn't already in the files there."

Christopher nodded. "I agree. It looks as though we're going to the Renaissance Faire."

CHAPTER FOUR

The Lexington Ren-Faire was located on the outermost fringes of the city, in that in between space before the lands around gave way to seemingly endless open fields and horse ranches. Paige could see several such ranches in the distance, along with what appeared to be a couple of race tracks. It seemed that everything in the area was given over to horses, although some of the skyscrapers back towards the center of the city suggested that there were plenty of other major businesses there as well.

Paige's eyes were more on the sprawl of the Renaissance Faire than on the city. It was strange to think that this one had become permanent, rather than moving around. It was bigger than she'd imagined it might be. Her mind's eye had conjured up somewhere small, maybe covering a single field. Instead, this was a large, meandering campus of a theme park, set behind large, arching black iron gates that seemed to have a deliberately handmade quality to them, as if they'd been produced by a medieval blacksmith rather than by machine and wanted to make sure that they showed it.

As she and Christopher approached those gates, there were already plenty of people lining up to get into the Renaissance Faire. There were families and groups of friends, couples, and people who had obviously come alone. Some of them were dressed in ordinary, casual clothes, but probably half or more were in costumes of various kinds. The majority of those costumes were interpretations of medieval dress that involved everything from a few items of old fashioned looking jewelry over otherwise simple clothes all the way up to what looked like full, homemade suits of armor. A few, though, had come in obvious fantasy costumes, or in costumes from other time periods, as if the whole place were one big playground for people who wanted to be different.

Paige realized the scale of the task facing her and Christopher when she saw that lots of them had weaponry of various kinds, too. There were people walking around with swords, and if most of them looked like they were plastic, at least a couple of them looked as though they weren't. Would one guy with a dagger stand out, in a situation like that?

Paige and Christopher walked up to the gates, with Paige doing her best to ignore the looks from the people there who thought that they were cutting the line. Paige showed her FBI badge to the greeter at the gate, a young man in what appeared to be the outfit of a knight, complete with large shield and longsword.

"FBI. We're here about Meredith Park."

Paige saw him swallow, looking worried as she said that. She took a guess.

"Did you know her?" Paige asked.

"Everyone did," the greeter replied. "She ran the restaurant. She got along with everyone."

"So she was popular?" Christopher asked, joining in.

They needed as much general information as they could get about Meredith if they were going to find answers in this case. In particular, they needed to know if anyone had a reason to hurt her. It was still possible that this was a double murder for some normal reason, rather than just because a serial killer had targeted them both.

The knight nodded. "When I wasn't on the gate, I would go help out around the park. I do some of the jousting shows and the mock combats. Meredith was always a good person. She had a smile for everyone, and she was always ready to do whatever she could to help."

"And where were you yesterday, when Meredith left the restaurant?" Christopher asked.

The knight on the gate hesitated as he tried to recall. "I was here. I was on the gate all day. You can check the schedule if you want."

"Hey, can we hurry things up here?" a guy called, from the line. He was standing there dressed like some homebrew Henry VIII, a big guy in a tunic, cloak, and ruff.

Paige wanted to know more about Meredith, but looking around, she could see that the other people in the line were getting a little impatient. She could find the information she needed elsewhere in the Faire.

"We should go in," Paige said.

Christopher led the way into the place, and Paige followed in his wake. It was even bigger in there than Paige had thought from the outside, with a number of buildings set out in rows, so that it seemed like a whole medieval village in the shadow of a small castle that looked like it had more to do with every TV fantasy series than with anything actually medieval. That castle had so many spires and turrets that it seemed like some great stone porcupine.

Quite a lot of the Renaissance Faire was open fields, though, punctuated by tents that looked semi-permanent, as if they'd been deliberately designed to create the impression of somewhere that had been thrown together for only a day or two when in fact they had sat there in the same spots for years. The field currently featured a couple of knights charging at each other on horseback while crowds roared their support, lances leveled, ready to knock one another off, and Paige heard the impact even from where she stood.

It felt strange to be dressed in suits here, given the number of people in many variations of medieval dress.

There were some in suits, too, although curiously old fashioned ones, often accompanied by goggles or homemade apparatus of brass and glass.

"Steampunk doesn't exactly fit the medieval feel," Christopher said, obviously seeing some of the same people.

"I get the feeling that historical accuracy isn't the main selling point of the Renaissance Faire," Paige replied. "I guess there's just something about it that encourages people's more creative sides to come out."

Which probably made it all a lot of fun to walk around under normal circumstances, but Paige wasn't there just to enjoy the atmosphere, and it also meant that asking the people there if they'd seen anything out of the ordinary yesterday might not give them many results. Even a man openly waving a strange knife around might not attract attention, since there was at least one performer with the Faire twirling a medieval Morningstar like it was a baton, sending the spiked head on a chain whirling around his body.

"We need to find the employee parking lot," Christopher said. "Once we get to the murder site, we can work out from there." He headed over to a large map of the Renaissance Faire, apparently carved out of a single cross-section of tree trunk, with details burned on it.

Paige could see the problem with it instantly: While it showed exactly where to go for the jousting field, the feasting hall, or King Arthur's Court, it didn't include the employee parking lot. This was a map for the customers, and presumably, whoever had designed the map hadn't thought that customers had any business there.

"We'll ask," Paige said, and headed over to where a man in tunic and hose was giving archery lessons to anyone who walked up, a trio of young people sending arrows flying out into straw targets a little way away. Or at least near those targets. They weren't all hitting very consistently.

"Have you come to try your hand and see if you're worthy of being one of King Arthur's yeomen?" the instructor asked.

"Actually, we wanted to ask you a couple of questions," Christopher said, stepping forward with his ID outstretched.

As soon as he saw the ID, the archery instructor's face fell, obviously knowing what this was going to be about. How could he not, with what had just happened?

"You're looking into what happened to Meredith?" he asked.

"We are," Paige said. "Did you know her?"

Everything about the way he reacted suggested that he had, just as the greeter at the gate had known her.

"Everyone knew Meredith," the archery instructor said. "She was one of those bright, bubbly people it's kind of hard to miss, even in a place like this."

"Did she have any enemies?" Christopher asked. It was a standard question, because sometimes, it was obvious to everyone around a victim who might have killed them.

Apparently not in this case, though.

"Enemies?" the archery instructor said. He sounded genuinely surprised by the idea. "No, of course not. Why would someone like Meredith have enemies?"

Paige suspected that he would be surprised how sometimes even the most ordinary people had enemies, but she needed to find another way to ask the question.

"But I'd guess that a place like this doesn't always run smoothly," Paige suggested. It was usually easier to get people to talk about any general trouble than it was to get them to admit that one of their friends had someone in their life who might want to kill them. People had often heard gossip that they didn't realize might be relevant.

"It's a Ren-Faire," the archery instructor said. "That means on an average day, we have the actors playing the knights not able to agree who should win their grand duel, a bunch of kids running through the place having their own mock battles that no one scheduled, people getting drunk because they don't get how strong mead is, arguments because *everyone* says they're a princess or a knight, people arguing about the historical accuracy of all of it…"

Meaning that even in a place like this that seemed as though it should be relatively carefree, there might be a bunch of arguments and unresolved conflicts lurking under the surface, any one of which might generate enough animosity for a killer to strike out at someone.

"Did you see Meredith last night, before she left to go home?" Christopher asked.

The archery instructor shrugged. "I saw her leaving. Plenty of people did. Meredith always understood that this is a show, so she always tried to make even leaving for the day as part of the performance."

"And you were here?" Paige asked, because the more people who they could establish locations for at the time Meredith was killed, the more chance there was of spotting anyone who wasn't where they should have been, or who lied about it.

He nodded. "There are always people wanting to shoot bows, right up to the minute we close the Faire. I had a group of tourists who had come to Kentucky for the horse racing, and decided to come over here for the afternoon."

"Thank you," Paige said. "Can you point us to the employee parking lot?"

"It's just over that way," the archery instructor said, jerking his head towards a spot behind several of the buildings that dominated the Renaissance Faire, one of them labelled "Royal Armory" and another labelled "Dungeon of Horrors."

Paige headed in the direction he'd indicated. It was still pretty early in the morning, but already the crowds were building up, and it didn't seem that anyone was put off by the news that someone had been murdered here. Certainly, none of the business seemed to be closed off or shut down in response to the situation.

The employee parking lot cordoned off with police tape that made it clear that no one was to pass, although there wasn't currently a forensics team there. In fact, there didn't seem to be any police presence at all, beyond one uniformed officer making sure that no one came in.

That confused Paige, because the crime scenes she'd been to in the past had been much busier places. She showed her badge to him as she and Christopher approached.

"Where is everyone?" she asked. There should have been a couple more officers around, at least.

The uniformed officer shrugged. "They just said to keep people out until the feds arrived. It's your case, and your crime scene, now."

Paige frowned at that, not understanding. On the last case she and Christopher had worked, the local police liaison had been more than helpful. They'd actually worked out of a local police precinct. If anything, the presence of the local detectives had been a little too much.

"This happens, sometimes," Christopher said. "The local PD doesn't want to put resources into a case once they know that the FBI is involved. They probably won't obstruct us, but they're not going to help us much either."

Meaning that she and Christopher were on their own. The thought of that made Paige a little nervous. It was just down to the two of them but then, it was always ultimately the two of them trying to solve cases and catch killers.

"It doesn't matter," Christopher said, sounding a lot more confident. "There's a field office in Lexington we can work out of. For now, I want to get a look at the crime scene."

He stepped past the tape, with Paige following in his wake, wondering what there really was to see there now that the body had been moved and any forensic team was gone.

"We can get an FBI forensics team in if we need one," Christopher said. "But I think the locals collected most of the evidence that was here. We'll get their evidence reports at least. I don't see any cameras covering the employee lot, but I saw a few as we passed through the main Faire."

That surprised Paige a little, seeming almost the wrong way around for a place that was selling people a taste of the past when they came there. But she guessed that it made a kind of sense that a place like this cared more about protecting its customers than it did about watching over the cars of its employees.

Would the killer have known that there were no cameras here? Had he picked this as a location for the murder because of that, knowing that there would be no evidence to show the world who had done it? Had he scouted it ahead of time? They would need to check for any sign of him on the camera footage the Renaissance Faire *did* have, but Paige had already seen the crowds out in the area. It would be hard to work out which of the people on any given camera shot was the one who had killed Meredith.

Paige could see Meredith Park's car there, a small silver Citroen, a few flecks of blood still visible above its wheel arches. Paige tried one of the doors and found it unlocked. Was that down to the forensics team, or had Meredith been trying to get into the safety of her car when she'd been killed?

Paige didn't know, but she found that she could at least picture the crime scene now that she was here. Meredith would have been lying... there, which meant that the killer must have approached from over... *there*.

"He came from inside the Renaissance Faire," Paige said. "Or at least, that's the direction he made his final approach from to kill her. If he'd come around from a different side, then Meredith wouldn't have been where she was while she was trying to get to her car."

"I agree," Christopher said. He was obviously reading the scene just as Paige was.

"I want to go back in there," Paige said. "It's possible that someone saw something, and I want to check up on that metal fleur-de-lis. It sounds like the kind of thing that might have some kind of connection to this place."

They headed back into the Renaissance Faire, back among the tents and the stalls, trying to find someone who might potentially know about the fleur-de-lis.

Paige saw a blacksmith working in front of an open air forge, while a stall next door sold the things that had been made there. The blacksmith was a heavily built man in his thirties, wearing a leather apron over his tunic and hose. He worked a set of bellows one handed, building up the flames of the forge to the point where he could put a billet of metal into it, softening it slowly so he could work on it. The space around him was filled with metal objects, from ornaments to candelabras, sections of railing to replica weapons.

He looked up as Paige and Christopher walked over. Paige showed her ID as they approached.

"What can I do for you, agents?" the blacksmith asked.

"We're looking into what happened to Meredith Park," Paige said. "Did you know her?"

"I saw her around," the blacksmith said, he sounded suddenly somber. "She was always friendly. I can't believe that anyone would want to kill her."

"Did you see her last night?" Christopher asked.

"I think I saw her as she was leaving," the blacksmith said. "I was busy putting on a demonstration for a group of kids, though."

"So did you see anyone watching her?" Christopher asked. "Anyone who was paying her too much attention, or seemed to be following her?"

"Like I said, I was doing a demo," the blacksmith said. "If you want to find anything like that, you'll probably have to check the security footage from the restaurant. They try to hide the cameras because it looks too 'modern,' but they're there."

Paige nodded. Christopher had already spotted a few of the cameras, and they would definitely need to check them for any sign of someone watching Meredith too closely in her workplace. That might point them at anyone who was stalking her.

Before they did that, though, she had a couple more questions. She called up an image of the fleur-de-lis ornament on her phone, holding it out for the blacksmith to look at.

"Have you seen something like this around here? Have you *made* something like this?"

The blacksmith shook his head, though.

"No. The fleur-de-lis is a pretty common symbol, though. It was used in France all the way back to its earliest Frankish kings. But around here, someone might just be using it because they think it's a nice symbol. Historical accuracy counts for nothing around here, but I don't think it's specifically anything to do with the Ren-Faire."

Paige had hoped that it would be something that it might be traced back here, but it seemed that the ubiquity of the symbol was too much. She should have known it wouldn't be that simple. There was one other thing she wanted to ask, though.

"You have a lot of different weapons around here," she said. "Have you ever heard of a dagger or a knife with a square sided blade, like a fire poker?"

She saw the blacksmith frown, as if that rang a faint bell for him.

"Maybe. I mean, I could do some research, try to find anything that fits that."

Paige gave him her number.

"Please call me if you think of anything," Paige said.

She'd been hoping that they might find more, but at least there was still a chance of getting information that might help.

For now, though, there was still a chance of getting something from the Renaissance Faire's security footage.

CHAPTER FIVE

Paige walked up to the restaurant. It was large and clad in fake stone, with battlements running along the line of the roof and windows that were leaded and stained, although the stained glass showed scenes that seemed more like something out of fantasy than anything that might have come up in real life, with images of knights and dragons running along most of the front.

Paige went inside with Christopher, and the whole place was still busy, with customers in every corner of the restaurant. There were families in booths and seated around large, rustic tables that looked like they'd been put together from roughhewn tree trunks, deliberately rough edged and not looking machine finished at all.

The walls were wood paneled, and there were elaborate weapons crossed on them behind shields whose designs seemed to have less to do with heraldry than simply the whims of whichever artist had worked on them. There were shields with whole painted landscapes and portraits, rather than just standard symbols. Each table had one huge, heavily carved, throne-like chair at its head so that someone in each group could play at being a king or queen, while all the glasses consisted of goblets and tankards. Even the lighting was arranged to look like old fashioned lanterns and burning torches on the walls. Wooden beams arched above them, along with tapestries that seemed to have been designed to depict fantastical battles.

"Hey!" a young woman serving as the greeter said. "Welcome, tired travelers, to our humble inn. The best in the kingdom. I'm Jessica. Can I show you to a table?"

She was short, only around Paige's height, with blonde hair and a heart shaped face. She was probably twenty-five, and was currently wearing a pale linen dress cinched at the waist by a dark corset, in what appeared to be an interpretation of medieval clothing filtered through years of Hollywood costumery.

Her greeting was bright enough, but Paige could see the strain on her face and the redness around her eyes, like she'd been crying recently. It was obvious that the news of Meredith's death had been affecting her.

"We're with the FBI," Paige said, showing her badge. "We're here about Meredith."

"Oh." That got a look of shock and worry, as if Jessica couldn't really work out how to respond to that.

Christopher intervened, obviously used to dealing with people still in shock after a death.

"Can we talk somewhere more private?" Christopher asked. "Maybe a back office?"

Jessica nodded hurriedly. "Yes, sorry, just this way."

She led the way past a door that had been painted to look as though there was a portcullis hanging over it, and which had a sign on it saying *Servants of the Kingdom Only.*

A surprisingly large and modern office space sat behind it, complete with several lockers that Paige guessed were for the staff to put any belongings in that didn't fit with the general medieval atmosphere of the place. The computer screen on a desk in the corner definitely didn't fit, and nor did the refrigerator that was presumably a place for the staff to put their own food. There were a couple of chairs there too, and Paige went with Christopher as he guided Jessica over to them.

"It's been… it's hard to believe that Meredith is actually gone," Jessica said. "Have you caught anyone yet?"

"Not yet," Christopher said, in a sympathetic tone, "but we won't stop looking. Were you here yesterday, Jessica?"

She shook her head in response. "I only cover the restaurant occasionally, when someone is sick. Normally, I work over in the soft play castle, for the younger kids."

"But you knew Meredith?" Paige asked. Given Jessica's reactions, it seemed impossible that she didn't. The two of them had obviously been friends.

"Everyone knew Meredith," Jessica said. "Everyone *liked* her. She was like the nicest person here."

"Did everyone share that opinion?" Paige asked. "Did anyone disagree with Meredith over anything?"

"No, of course not," Jessica said, as if she couldn't even conceive of the possibility of someone hating the dead woman. Paige had noticed that often seemed to be people's reaction to death, so that even if there was some part of someone's life that might have resulted in arguments, they ignored it.

In this case, though, it fit with what Paige had heard from other people. It seemed that she really was well loved around the Renaissance Faire, to a degree that made it impossible for people to believe that anyone might want to kill Meredith. Which meant that either there was something hidden deeper that had gotten her killed, or they really were dealing with a serial killer for whom some linking factor between the victims was all he needed to spark him into killing.

That possibility was in some ways the most terrifying because it would mean that there was nothing in Meredith or Gisele's lives that Paige could link back to the killer. There would be no way to find him just by looking closer at them. It also meant that other women might find themselves killed for almost no reason at all.

That was if it was that kind of serial killer. It was still more than possible that this was someone who simply had a well-hidden reason to hate both Meredith and Gisele. Finding *that* out meant looking closer, trying to find any link between the two victims and hoping that they would be able to follow that link all the way back to the killer's door.

"Did you see Meredith at all yesterday?" Paige asked.

Jessica shook her head, though. "I was working at the other side of the Faire. It can get pretty busy here, especially when it's the season for the big knight tournaments."

"Knight tournaments?" Paige said.

"We put on jousting displays and displays of medieval combat, but we also host tournaments for them. Pro jousters and Historical European Martial Arts experts come in to prove that they're the best. People like it, because they know that there's something real to it, you know?"

Paige had been only vaguely aware that such things existed until Jessica explained it. It sounded impressive to her, but right then, it wasn't relevant to the case if Meredith hadn't been a part of those aspects of the Renaissance Faire. For now, though, Paige and Christopher needed to check the most obvious source of evidence available to them. The one that people had already mentioned.

"Jessica, is there security footage for the restaurant?" Paige asked, trying to keep her tone gentle.

The waitress nodded. "People get out of hand sometimes, trying to have mock battles in the restaurant. Plus, we've had some problems with property damage. So there are cameras watching everything, in case we need to call the cops."

"Can we look at that footage?" Paige asked. "Do you have access to it?"

She saw Jessica nod, obviously determined to be helpful.

"We all get access to the footage for the areas where we work. If you want the footage for the whole faire, you'll have to send a request to the king's court."

"The king's court?" Christopher asked, sounding slightly confused.

Jessica shook her head, obviously realizing that not everywhere used the same jargon as the Renaissance Faire staff. "Sorry, it's what we call the management here. They thought it would fit in with the atmosphere. So we have a chief herald instead of a head of marketing, and a chief wizard instead of a head of IT."

It sounded to Paige like the kind of thing that would be amusing and interesting the first few times one heard it, but that might get a bit much after a while. It was as if everything there at the Renaissance Faire had to fit in with the image that it was looking for, and that in turn pointed to more of a corporate side than Paige had expected from somewhere like this.

"The security footage from the restaurant should be enough to start with," Christopher said. "Can you call it up for us?"

Jessica nodded, and then went over to the computer, typing in a password and then turning the screen so that Paige and Christopher could use it.

"This will have everything from the restaurant," Jessica said. "You might be able to download it if you need it. Like I said, I can't really give you anything from the rest of the Faire."

"That's great," Christopher said, with a charming smile that Paige found herself wishing were directed her way before she stopped herself. "I guess you need to get back to work?"

Jessica nodded. "Just shout if you need anything."

She left, and Paige guessed that Christopher wanted that space in order to be able to go through the security footage without an audience. He called it up on the screen, a couple of cameras providing different angles on the restaurant, showing all the waitresses and the customers.

"Do you want to make a start on this?" Christopher asked. "I'll make a call and see if I can get the rest of the footage from around the Renaissance Faire. Although I'll have to send it over to the techs back at Quantico. There's likely to be a lot of footage, and I don't want the two of us tied down searching through it."

Paige nodded. Maybe with the skills she'd built up as a psychologist, she would be well placed to pick out anyone who was giving Meredith the wrong kind of attention.

She scrolled back through the footage, looking for any sign of Meredith, since she was interested in anyone who was in the room at the same time. Paige found the point where she left the restaurant, waving to the diners there almost as if she were an actor leaving the stage after a well-received performance in a play. She scrolled back before that, stopping and starting the recording to catch different fragments, watching Meredith as she went about her shift.

Would the killer have been in there? Would he have watched her and followed her? It was definitely possible, *particularly* if Paige assumed that this was a case where the killer had identified her as a victim relatively soon before he killed her. Yes, there were other moments when she'd been walking through the Faire and someone might have picked her out, but the restaurant had been the place where she'd spent most of her day. It seemed like the most likely spot for someone to have decided to kill her, if they didn't already have some kind of grudge against her.

Maybe even then. After all, the killer could have been sitting in there, waiting for his moment. In any case, it meant that there was a chance for Paige to try to spot the killer as he stalked her. That was behavior that Paige was confident she could pick out, and it might give her and Christopher a chance to catch the killer before he had a chance to strike again.

Paige started to look over the footage, but now that she'd found Meredith in it, she didn't keep her attention on the waitress. Instead, Paige watched the people around her in the footage, carefully scanning the groups there as Meredith moved between them, looking for anyone who didn't seem to react in any of the normal ways that people did around wait staff.

Paige was watching their body language, trying to pick out anyone who was paying Meredith more attention than they should, or looking at her with obvious signs of aggression. She tried to narrow down her search a little, working out who she needed to pay attention to. Basic psychological principles helped her to eliminate some people as potential suspects, based on body language or behavior.

Would it be someone in a group? Paige didn't think so, because this was someone who'd needed to be alone in order to kill. Someone in a group would have had to make an excuse to go off without the others they were with. That would potentially expose them to being caught if their friends went looking for them, and that would be too much danger for most killers.

No, someone about to kill would be alone. That narrowed down the number of people Paige needed to look at considerably. People tended to come to the Renaissance Fair in groups.

She found one person watching Meredith, her attention caught by the relative stillness of him against the crowd. It was a man in his thirties, wearing a suit rather than anything that fit in with the medieval theme of the Renaissance Faire. He was tall and thin faced, quite good looking, and he seemed to be looking at Meredith with a note of curiosity as he sat alone at a table. There was something close to obsession there on his features, something that made Paige keep staring at him for a minute or more.

He didn't do anything, though, didn't approach her, didn't talk to her, certainly didn't argue with her. As far as Paige could see, he was just one more customer among the others, waiting for his waitress to come over and take his order. Maybe she was wrong about his expression because he quickly faded into the background again. Certainly, the way he looked at Meredith didn't seem like enough to keep going with.

Paige kept looking, searching for any hint of an altercation, anything that might point to someone who was building up to attacking Meredith. Surely, as a waitress, she had to deal with rowdy customers occasionally? Maybe even be firm with them to stop them from causing damage or upsetting the other customers.

Yet Paige couldn't find anyone there who looked like they had any kind of problem with Meredith. There was no one who had picked a fight, no instance where she had to break up an altercation, or stop them from acting in a way they shouldn't. There simply wasn't any sign of conflict on the footage Paige had.

"How's it going?" Christopher asked, coming over.

"Did you get the footage?" Paige asked.

"They're sending it through to our techs," Christopher said. "If there's anything there, they'll let us know."

Paige hoped so. The FBI's techs were good at their jobs, but would they be able to identify the subtle behavioral cues that said someone was thinking of killing Meredith? That was the danger with leaving it to others: Paige couldn't be sure that they had the same skillset as her.

"Was there anyone on the footage who looked like they might be the killer?" Christopher asked.

Paige shook her head. "There's no one who had a problem with her that I could… wait."

Paige pointed to the screen as a figure briefly walked across. He was obviously looking Meredith's way, unable to take his eyes from her.

That wasn't the part that made Paige pause, though. That had more to do with the part where she recognized the figure there. It was someone who shouldn't have been there, someone who certainly hadn't *admitted* to being anywhere near Meredith when they'd talked to him.

"Isn't that the guy from the entrance?" Paige asked. "The one in the knight's outfit?"

It was; Paige was sure that it was. He was standing there, staring at Meredith, when he'd claimed that he was on the gate all day, and had said that he was nowhere near her when she died. He'd lied about where he'd been, and that made Paige curious. What else hadn't he told them? Why had he tried to hold back where he'd been yesterday? Was it because he'd been busy killing Meredith, and was even now trying to find a way to hide it?

Whatever the reason, Paige and Christopher needed to talk to him, right away.

CHAPTER SIX

Paige and Christopher hurried towards the entrance where they'd first met the guy in the knight's costume, with Paige feeling a growing sense of anxiety. When they got to the entrance, would the man in the knight's costume try to fight? Would he run? Had he *already* run, seeing the arrival of the FBI at the Renaissance Faire as his cue to get as far away as possible? Paige suspected that it wouldn't be the latter, if he hadn't run already, but she knew that she had to be ready now for whatever happened. If this was the killer, then they couldn't let him get away to kill again.

They reached the gates at something close to a run. The waiting lines of people there were still out in front, trying to get in. Paige was more interested in the greeter, though, ready to confront the man in the knight's costume that she had just seen in the video.

Only he wasn't there in the spot he'd been in before. Instead, there seemed to be a jester taking people's money and letting them into the Faire, making wisecracks at their expense as he did so and occasionally juggling. Paige went up to him anyway.

"Where's the guy who was on the gate?" she asked, in an urgent tone.

"Marry, nuncle," he said with a playful expression that Paige guessed was well practiced, "how strange your mode of speech is. And your dress. Most unfitting for a wench of King Arthur's court."

The jester was obviously playing a part he'd played plenty of times with anyone who looked too modern for the general dress code of the Faire, but Paige didn't have time for it right then. She had a suspect to catch, and the man in the knight's costume could already be running.

Paige took out her badge and repeated her question slowly and carefully, leaving no room for the jester to think that this was a game.

"The guy who was on the gate before you, where is he?"

"Marry, nuncle…" the jester began, and only then seemed to fully take in the badge in front of him. The playfulness fell out of his expression, fading into something far more serious and worried. "FBI? Seriously? And you want to talk to Steve?"

"What's his full name?" Christopher asked, obviously wanting to be able to get details on their suspect even if they couldn't catch him right away.

"Steve... Baker, I think," the jester said. "Sorry, we don't use a lot of surnames. He's over at the jousting at the moment. He's not like the top guy, but the crowds like him. He plays the black knight pretty well."

The jousting meant the large churned up field in front of the Renaissance Faire's fake castle. Paige and Christopher made for it as fast as they could, covering the ground at something close to a run, and found a growing crowd heading that way too, albeit at a slower pace. The crowd was filling up wooden stands emblazoned with the colors and heraldic devices of different jousters, presumably to give them a sense of rooting for one knight or another.

Another stand sat opposite, more of a stage than a true watching platform, there to house a couple of figures seated on elaborate thrones, plus their servants and heralds. It was obviously a part of the show, although a couple of VIP guests also seemed to be up there. Paige found herself wondering just how much they'd paid to be up there.

The space between held a long railing to separate the jousters, adorned with flags, with knights clustered at either end, waiting for their turns to charge at one another down the lists. They paced and adjusted the straps of their armor. Not everything was quite so medieval, though: a small golf cart was making its way around the crowd, selling refreshments to the watching spectators, and a jester was using a t-shirt cannon to fire clothing out into the stands.

Even as Paige stood there, two figures on horseback came out, their armor shining so bright that it almost hurt her eyes to look their way, their shields emblazoned with a sun and a bear. Their horses were huge and covered in armor of their own, the barding displaying the same heraldic devices as the shields. Their hooves pawed at the ground as they stood waiting at the end of the lists and they snorted as if eager for the fray.

"And now," a figure on one of the thrones boomed, obviously assisted by a hidden speaker system, "the magnificent knight of the sun will take on the knight of the bear, for the favor of Lady Gwendoline!"

Paige saw the two of them level their lances, lowering them towards one another with hostile intent, their horses charging towards one another at speed. At the last minute, both knights ducked down behind their shields, angling their lances to try to strike a clean blow on one another while they tried to keep their heads out of the way of the impact. The sound of that impact was like a thunderclap, loud enough to fill the open space in front of the castle, and Paige saw splinters fly in every direction as the two lances snapped. One of the knights went tumbling from his horse in the midst of that shower of fragments, hitting the ground hard and rolling as he did so.

He came up, and now he seemed to be taunting the other knight with deliberately large, obvious gestures that the crowd would understand, drawing a longsword two-handed as he did so and flourishing it to get an appreciative sound from the crowd. The other knight turned and dismounted, keeping his shield and drawing a mace that looked heavy and violent. The two of them stalked one another for a few seconds, feinting and threatening.

Then, they started to exchange blows in what was obviously a carefully choreographed sequence, complete with jumps and rolls that saw the weapons missing the two combatants by inches. The one with the longsword seemed to be aiming for the shield of the one with the mace, while the mace wielder seemed to be telegraphing his blows to make sure that his opponent had enough time to deal with them. The crowd cheered each attempt, but now Paige wasn't concentrating on the fight. Instead, she was making her way over to where the knights and squires were gathered, her eyes seeking out Steve Baker. He had to be there somewhere.

She caught her first glimpse of him there grooming a large black horse, checking the cinch on his saddle as he got ready for his own turn in front of the crowd. Paige started to make her way over to him faster now, but even as she did so, she saw him mounting up, grabbing a lance stuck into a rack of them and pulling a full-faced helmet down over his features as he got ready to joust.

"I've looked up Steve Baker," Christopher said, holding up his phone. He'd obviously logged in to the FBI's systems to run a search on their suspect, wanting to know everything about him. "He has a record, for stalking an ex-girlfriend. There were some suggestions that he'd been violent, although that wasn't proven."

A stalker with a possible history of violence? Paige wanted to talk to him even more. Now, he wasn't just a guy who'd lied to them about where he was; he was a guy with a record of potential violence who had lied to them, and who might well have lashed out, given the right provocation.

She and Christopher were pretty close now, maybe twenty feet away from the area reserved for the knights, approaching as Steve got ready to go out and joust. Paige considered letting him get that over with before they talked to him, and then catching him once he was done, but this couldn't wait. He'd lied to them about being at the gate all yesterday, and Paige wanted to know why. There was no time to waste.

"Steve Baker!" she called out as she and Christopher got close, wanting to catch his attention and get him to come down off the horse. She flashed her badge.

Paige saw him look her way, turning in her direction, his expression impossible to read. Paige couldn't see his face because of the helmet, but she could imagine the look of worry and surprise there in that moment. She'd seen that look on the face of suspects before.

"We need to ask you some questions about Meredith, and about why you lied to us!"

Paige quickly realized her mistake, however, as Steve wheeled his horse, lance still clutched in his hand. She'd panicked him, and now he was going to try to run, try to get away from the FBI. On foot, that would have been fine, because they could simply have chased, but Steve had a horse, and there was no way that Paige was going to be able to keep up with him on foot, in spite of the conditioning that came from Paige's FBI training.

People threw themselves out of the way of the horse, because something that big, moving that fast, was a potential risk to anyone in its path. There was a low fence in the way, but the horse cleared it easily, heading out across the jousting ground without any concern for anyone in the way.

"It seems we have some excitement from the dark knight!" the actor playing the king said, obviously trying to incorporate the sudden disruption into the bigger act, as if this were the kind of thing that happened every day. Maybe he was used to horses not doing what they were meant to. "His fear of our knights is so great that he... what *is* he doing?"

He was getting away, that was what he was doing. Paige looked around for a way to chase him, and her eyes fell on the other horses there, but Paige had no pretentions of being an expert rider. She'd been on a horse a couple of times in her life, at best. Certainly, she wasn't going to be good enough to keep up with someone who spent half his life on a horse, jousting and playing up to the crowd.

Paige found herself looking for another solution to the problem, looking around, trying to find anything that might be faster than a horse. Christopher had already found an answer of his own. He was running over to the small golf cart that they used for the catering, his badge already out.

"FBI! I need this vehicle, right now!" he yelled.

He put such authority into his tone that the driver didn't even argue, just leapt out of the driver's seat at speed, trying to get clear. The spectators actually applauded, as if they thought that all of this was a part of the show that had been scheduled from the start.

Christopher drove over with the golf cart, the cart moving with a strange, electric speed, and Paige leaped aboard while it was still moving, grabbing on for dear life as Steve Baker headed in the opposite direction and they followed.

"Do you really think this will be able to keep up with a horse?" Paige asked, still trying to hang onto the gold cart.

"There's only one way to find out."

Christopher hit the gas pedal as he said it. He sent the golf cart hurtling forward after Steve, the would-be knight, darting through a gap in the fence around the jousting field and following along in his wake at surprising speed. Certainly faster than any horse in a straight line.

The golf cart was, Paige had to admit, a lot faster than she'd thought it would be. It was also bumpy and unstable, the ruts of the field bouncing it around as if it might flip over at any moment. It felt like a small boat bounced on the waves of a giant sea, and Paige clung on tight, trying to tell herself that a golf cart was *designed* for this kind of off road work.

Steve was still ahead on his horse, riding hard. He was zigzagging now, changing direction apparently at random, as if trying to make it harder for Paige and Christopher to guess which way he was going from moment to moment. He still had the lance in his hand, but Paige was more worried about the sword and shield strapped across his back, obviously there for some stage fight after his bout. Those would be the weapons he would attack them with, given the chance. Paige didn't know if that sword would be sharp or not. She doubted it, since everything here was for show, but could she really risk it when this was someone she suspected of having killed two women?

Paige thought about the gun at her side. She'd been trained to use it; had sent thousands of rounds downrange in the course of her training, ready for exactly this kind of moment. Steve was armed, and was currently looking like more and more of a suspect in two murders. Should she fire? That was the kind of decision that Paige had been told from the start of her training that she would have to make.

No, Paige decided as Steve continued to try to make his escape on horseback, he might be trying to run, but he didn't currently represent a threat to her, Christopher, or any innocent civilians. She couldn't just shoot him because he was running, not when he wasn't potentially about to hurt anyone.

Besides, on a more practical level, Paige wasn't sure that she would be able to hit him if she tried. The bullet could go anywhere, with the way that the golf cart was bouncing and weaving over the broken ground of the field, churned up by so many horses' hooves that it was more like a muddy obstacle course than a flat field. The golf cart bounced left and right, so that there would be no chance of Paige getting a clear shot.

Now, Steve was riding his horse in a straight line, racing across the field at a gallop, trying to put as much distance as possible between himself and the cart. It wasn't a race horse, though, and the armor slowed it down, so the golf cart was at least keeping pace, even gaining on him slowly over the broken ground.

Not fast enough. Paige could see the reason now that he'd started to race away so directly, rather than continuing to zigzag. There was a small patch of woodland ahead, and at the rate that the horse was moving, it would make it there before the golf cart got close enough to try to stop it. Once into the woodland, the horse would be able to move through the trees much faster than the golf cart could, simply being more agile in such a confined space. Steve would be able to lose them, and once he did, there was no guarantee that they would find him again.

He would be free to kill again, if he wanted to do so. He might even accelerate, knowing that he was being hunted.

Paige had to think of a way to stop him before he got to the trees, and now she could think of one that might actually achieve something. She got out her gun.

"You can't just shoot someone for running," Christopher said, in an obviously worried tone.

"I don't need to shoot him," Paige replied, hoping that she was correct, and fired twice, deliberately aiming above both Steve and his horse.

The sound filled the space around them. It was enough to startle the horse, and now, instead of running, it was wheeling, looking for the sound. Paige fired once more, straight up, startling it so that it reared in fear, whinnying in sudden, uncontrollable panic.

The suddenness of the movement was too much for Steve when he wasn't expecting it. He tried to cling to his reins as the horse reared beneath him, but with one hand still holding onto the lance, he simply couldn't hold on long enough. He lost his grip.

He went tumbling backwards off the horse, his armor clattering heavily as he hit the ground in a heap. Paige was already leaping from the golf cart as Christopher pulled it alongside the fallen man. The horse had decided to run again now, heading for the trees once more without the restricting weight of its rider.

Steve, meanwhile, was reaching for the sword at his back as if he might be able to use it to fight back against his pursuers. Paige moved in quickly, determined to get there before he could clear the weapon from its sheath and bring it to bear. She reached Steve, wrenching his arm and pulling him over onto his stomach with all her weight behind the movement.

She kicked away the sword, sending it skidding away over the dirt. She quickly searched him for other weapons, the way she'd been trained to do back at Quantico. A part of her hoped that he would be carrying a dagger that fit the weapon profile the coroner had set out, proving beyond doubt that this was the killer she'd been looking for. To her disappointment, there was nothing like that, but she still set handcuffs around Steve's wrists.

"Steve Baker, you're under arrest."

CHAPTER SEVEN

Because they weren't working with the local police on this case, the way they had with some of the murders they'd investigated previously, Paige and Christopher took Steve Baker to the nearest FBI field office for questioning. It was a small, modern looking building in Lexington, more like the offices of a firm of accountants than a place for federal law enforcement, with a parking facility nearby and a series of glass fronted offices set out one on top of another.

To Paige's surprise, even though she guessed that it shouldn't have been a surprise, there were reporters waiting outside of the field office, crowding around as if they might not even let Paige and Christopher through without a fight. The moment Paige and Christopher stepped out of the car with Steve, the reporters pressed in close, taking pictures and shouting out questions, each of them trying to be the one who got an answer.

"Agents, have you caught the killer?" one of them called out, leaning in with a microphone while a camera operator focused on Steve Baker. "Is this the man who killed Meredith Park and Gisele Newbury?"

"Can you reassure the people of Lexington that they're safe?" another shouted, pressing forward.

"Are you actually making any progress?"

The questions jabbed out like sharp points towards the three of them, leaving no real space for Paige or Christopher to actually answer, only trying to rachet up the pressure until something happened that might be newsworthy.

"Inquiries are ongoing," Christopher said, in a carefully neutral tone that gave away nothing. It was a tone Paige had heard him use before, with other reporters.

"We'll make a statement later," Paige tried, in an attempt to persuade them that they might get an answer if they were just sufficiently patient. It at least got them to back off enough that they could walk Steve towards the door, through a brief, empty corridor between the waiting cameras. The reporters didn't try to follow them in, and Paige dared to breathe a sigh of relief once she was inside.

The interior of the building seemed vaguely like that of a carefully designed lawyer's office to Paige. Inside, the whole place was bright and clean, but without the kind of expense that went into things at Quantico. Most of it really did just look like an office, except that the office workers poring over files there would be trained FBI agents and techs, there to help catch the worst criminals, and most of them would be armed, ready for any trouble.

Paige and Christopher put Steve in an interrogation room that looked more like a therapist's room from Paige's previous job at the St. Just Institute for the criminally insane, filled with soft furnishings and painted in pastel colors. Paige understood that the idea was to create a less confrontational environment where a suspect might be more willing to talk, but even so, it felt jarring after spending time in harsher environments. It felt wrong, somehow, compared to the time she'd spent in prisons with tables bolted to the floor.

They ran more background checks on the would-be knight while they waited for his lawyer to show up, since they wouldn't be able to talk to him until then. Paige saw the same charges relating to harassment that Christopher had mentioned, looking over the details of the stalking, the way Steve had kept showing up at his ex's house long after she'd asked him to stop, harassing her and claiming that he wanted to get back together with her. There were a couple of side notes of her alleging that he'd struck her on one of those unwanted visits, but those hadn't formed a part of the conviction or the restraining order, because there hadn't been enough corroborating evidence to make the charges stick.

Paige looked through what she could find of his social media next, picking through the public side of it as carefully as she could, trying to find anything that would get through to him and thus serve to get some answers out of their suspect. She mostly found posts about his work at the Ren-Faire, with plenty of videos of him jousting or fighting, showing off for the crowds. He obviously loved playing the part of the dark knight.

Paige started to look through those videos with a purpose, trying to find any glimpse of Meredith in them. She wasn't in most of them, because she would have been busy with her work at the restaurant, but Paige kept looking. In a couple, she was there, on the fringes of the crowd, helping with the catering. In both of them, Steve was looking her way, with an expression that Paige could only describe as longing.

"Is it my imagination," Paige said, "or is Steve staring at Meredith like some kind of lovesick puppy in both of these?"

Christopher came over, looking through the videos that Meredith had found.

"It's not your imagination," Christopher said, although if he could spot that look in Steve, it raised the worrying possibility that he could also see it whenever Paige looked his way. It wasn't as if she could just turn off the attraction that she felt towards him, and it was obvious that he'd seen it before on her face.

For now though, Paige forced herself to focus on the job.

Steve Baker's weapons were set out to one side of the office that she and Christopher were using, laid out on a table, waiting for their inspection. Paige went over to that table, trying to see if there was anything there that might potentially have made the wounds that Meredith and Giselle suffered. She was looking for anything thin and sharp, square sided and pointed.

Not the lance or the sword, obviously, because they were far too large to have done it. There was a dagger too, but this was a broad bladed, single edged affair almost as long as Paige's forearm. A brief piece of research on her phone suggested that it was called a "messer" and it definitely wasn't a candidate to have caused the wounds that killed the two women. It was completely the wrong shape. As for the shield and a couple of spiked pauldrons, they seemed more decorative and defensive than like something that could be used to kill in the way the serial killer had.

Maybe that meant that Steve had disposed of his weapon of choice, or maybe he kept it somewhere else, so that no one would spot it until he was ready to use it. Possibly he didn't routinely carry it as a part of his knightly uniform, although the absence troubled Paige at least a little.

"I think his lawyer is here," Christopher said, looking at a message on his phone that must have come through from the field office's front desk to give him a heads up. "Come on, we'll meet them in the interview room."

"What do you think it means that the local PD aren't liaising with us on this case?" Paige asked. That part of all this still bothered her a little. "I know you said before that it happens sometimes, but it still feels weird."

She heard Christopher sigh.

"My guess is that they're hoping we'll fail," Christopher said, with a note of disappointment. "They're pissed that the FBI is involved, and the best way they can show that is to refuse to do anything to help. Then they tell the local press about our involvement, so that if we get anything wrong, they can emphasize that they'd be doing a much better job. It's all just politics."

Politics. The local cops refusing to help, and hoping that they would mess up in the middle of looking for a serial killer, and it was just politics? Paige couldn't accept that. They should all be out there, working together, trying to catch a killer. The need to look good shouldn't come into it.

Paige just had to hope that they could get something out of Steve Baker. With the way that he'd run, she had to feel a sense of hope that he might be the killer. He was clearly obsessed with Meredith. One look at him from the security footage had Paige convinced of that. Maybe he'd been just as obsessed with Gisele. Maybe that was what happened with him now: he stalked victims, and when they gave the least sign of rejecting him, he killed them with some unknown weapon that he'd picked up as part of his job as a knight at the Renaissance Faire.

It was plausible. Now, she and Christopher just needed to find out if there was any actual evidence to prove it.

She and Christopher went into the interrogation room, and found Steve in conversation with a middle aged man in a cheap suit who Paige assumed had to be his lawyer. Steve was still wearing the remnants of his armor, minus anything that might be used to inflict an injury. He looked far too hot and uncomfortable in it now that he wasn't on the jousting field. Was that just about being indoors, or did it have more to do with him slowly becoming aware of the level of trouble he was in?

Paige and Christopher took chairs nearby, taking the time to consider Steve's reaction to their presence. Whereas some suspects had a lot of bluster and anger to them, Steve looked nervous, and seemed to be looking over to his lawyer for support, as if hoping that the lawyer would just hand him a way out of all of this without him having to say anything to anyone. Paige looked up to where a camera was watching proceedings, wanting to make sure that everything was recorded properly for this.

"So, Steve," Christopher asked once they were in position in the interrogation room, "why did you run from us?"

"I… I just panicked, that's all." There was an edge of fear even now in his voice.

"You just panicked?" Paige said. She didn't believe it for a moment.

"The two of you coming towards me like that, so soon after everything that had happened, I just assumed…"

He tailed off, as if realizing that whatever he'd assumed wasn't about to show him in a good light. Paige could see how someone might be worried by the FBI coming after them, but to take off on horseback like that? To run while endangering people? No, there was something more here than just natural nerves around authority. Paige wanted to know what it was.

"You assumed what, Steve?" Paige asked. "That we knew that you'd lied to us?"

"You don't have to answer that," his lawyer said.

"I didn't…"

Christopher stepped in before he could complete the lie. "You told us that you hadn't seen Meredith Park the day she died, and you implied that you were nowhere near her at the time she left her job."

"That was all just a misunderstanding," Steve said, in a worried tone, looking across at his lawyer as if the man would make the evidence go away.

"We have security footage from the restaurant showing that you were there just before she left yesterday," Paige said. "You were looking her way. You even spoke to her."

"That's not a crime," Steve said.

Christopher shook his head. "No, it isn't, but lying to the FBI in the middle of an investigation?"

"You have no evidence that my client deliberately lied to you," the lawyer said. "You say that he said that he was nowhere near Meredith Park, but we only have your word for that."

Christopher went on as if the lawyer hadn't spoken. "At the very least, that's suspicious. Why didn't you want us to know that you'd seen Meredith just before her death? Why did you decide that you needed to hide that, unless you had something to do with her death?"

Paige watched Steve's face as Christopher made the accusation, trying to read any change in his expression. She could see the shock there, and the sudden fear. Was he afraid that he'd been found out, or simply afraid because of the enormity of what he was being accused of? It was hard for Paige to tell. That was the problem with trying to read faces: the same emotion could be sparked by many different things. He certainly didn't look like he wanted to be there, but who *would* want to be in an FBI interrogation room?

"I didn't... I *couldn't*," he said. "I *loved* her!"

That didn't mean anything. Someone sufficiently obsessed could easily believe that he loved someone even while he killed her. Many people each year were killed by people who would swear afterwards that they loved the victim, and they meant it.

"The way you loved the woman you were arrested for harassing?" Paige asked.

The lawyer coughed. "I understood that we were discussing matters pertaining to yesterday."

"A history of harassing women sounds like it might be relevant to the death of another woman who had become the object of your client's attentions," Christopher said.

Steve shook his head. "That... that was different. Pamela never understood me."

"But you still thought that you loved her, didn't you?" Paige said. "You still stalked her, showing up at her house, and her place of work. The way you showed up at the restaurant just to see Meredith."

Steve was shaking his head. "You're making it sound... wrong. It wasn't like that."

"What was it like?" Paige asked. "The police reports suggest that it was obsessive, and even violent..."

"I never hurt her! I never hurt anyone!"

Steve was on his feet now in his armor. Paige and Christopher stood too, ready for trouble.

"Sit down, please," Christopher said, with a firm note in his voice. Even though Paige was sure that she could take down Steve if she had to, it was good to know that Christopher was there and had her back.

"Sit down," his lawyer said.

Reluctantly, the Ren-Faire knight settled back into place, and Paige considered her next questions.

"You say that you loved Meredith," she said. "Was that love reciprocated?"

"I... I only asked her out the day she died," Steve said. "She was pretty busy, so we hadn't even worked out a good time to meet up."

Suggesting to Paige that she'd rejected Steve, however gently. It certainly seemed possible that someone sufficiently obsessed my take that as his cue to kill. Steve's link to Meredith was unquestionable,

45

along with his potential motive. Add in the fact that he'd lied about where he was, and that he'd run, and he looked pretty suspicious. Once they started to look into his life, Paige felt pretty confident that they would find more, certainly about his obsession. They could try to get a warrant and search his home, anywhere he might hide a weapon that matched the wounds. If they found that, then they would have him.

First, though, Paige wanted to establish any connection Steve had to Gisele Newbury. This was a killer who had murdered *two* victims, not one.

"Tell me about Gisele," she said, watching for a reaction. That was more important than Steve's words.

"Who?"

"Gisele Newbury. She was found dead by her car two days ago. Where were you, the day before yesterday, at 5pm?"

Steve looked over to his lawyer, who nodded.

"I was out in Lexington. It was my day off. I went to a restaurant. You can check."

Meaning that he'd been in front of a whole crowd of people at the time when Gisele was killed. More than that, it was an alibi that she and Christopher would be able to check relatively easily, just by calling the restaurant. It meant he couldn't have killed Gisele.

"We'll need the name of the restaurant, and any receipts you got there," Christopher said. Paige could sense the disappointment in his voice.

It matched Paige's. If what Steve was saying was true, then he couldn't be Gisele's killer, and the odd shape of the stab wounds in both cases meant that it was almost certainly one killer.

A killer who was currently out there somewhere, and who might kill again soon if Paige and Christopher didn't find him.

CHAPTER EIGHT

He was not in his usual conveyance as he made his way around the city. No, for today, he was wandering Lexington in his own way, ignoring the occasional looks he got from lesser folks who glanced his way. He wanted to experience his city fully, and let people see that he was better than they were.

It was natural that they should look on their betters with awe. It wasn't their fault if their place in the grand scheme of things was simply… less. So long as they understood that, and paid him his proper deference, all was well. The natural order of things was maintained.

He walked with a light step for now, taking in the day around him, feeling a hint of joy and power at the memory of the things he'd done in the last couple of days. The weight of his weapon of justice was there at the small of his back, hidden beneath his clothing so as not to provoke any difficulties. He didn't want difficulties; he simply wanted the world around him to work as it should, as it *must*.

He just wanted people to acknowledge his superior place in the grand scheme of things. The realtor had failed to, and the waitress. They had paid the price for that failure, and there was only one price great enough for it: death.

He stopped to wait for a bus, a line of people already waiting there. They didn't acknowledge his presence, and if they looked his way with a hint of resentment as he made his way to the front of that line, none of them said anything. That deference was enough for him, for now.

He had learned a long time ago that the world was not the equal place it claimed to be. He suspected that he'd been born knowing it, deep in his bones. People were not born equal, were not the same as one another, did not have rights and privileges, whatever fiction they told themselves about it. The truth was that some were just born greater, and it fell to others to acknowledge that, or the great system of the world failed.

He was, of course, better than any of the rest of them. Smarter, stronger, simply better in every way. Even with people who appeared to be clever, or rich, or powerful, there was an indefinable essence to him that just made him… *more.* That much had been revealed to him years ago, the moment he'd first read about the order and structure of the medieval world. He had never doubted the truth of it since.

The bus came, at last, running several minutes late. That inconvenience was the first small insult, but at least the driver smiled as he graced the conveyance with his presence, and told him to have a nice day, the way such a servant should.

The problem came when he stepped past the driver to find the bus nearly full. There were no seats that did not have at least one person in them, and most were filled with two. He preferred a seat to himself, or certainly one where there was enough room for him to spread out properly. The idea of having to share his space was deeply annoying.

He picked one close to the front, the ideal spot. *His* spot. Only there was a woman sitting there, young and spikey-haired, dressed most inappropriately in jeans and a leather jacket more suited to a man, listening to music on a set of headphones, while taking up more of the seat than she should.

He stood before her, waiting for her to acknowledge his presence as she ought to. Yet it took almost a minute before she even looked up.

"Yeah, what do you want?"

"I require my seat." He said it with the authority of the man he knew he was, an authority that should have made this peasant practically leap from her spot to concede it.

"Your seat?" The young woman snorted. "Does this seat have your name on it?"

"I *require* my *seat*," he repeated, anger growing in him at the insubordination. "Do you know who I am?"

"Don't know, don't care," the young woman said. She deliberately spread out even more, making it clear that he wasn't going to be getting any part of the seat without a fight. Maybe not even then.

His anger made him want to reach for his weapon, there and then, to strike her down, to kill her so that the others would see it and fall back from him in fear…

The only problem with that was that far too many of the rest of the world didn't acknowledge him the way they should, either. Already, he had seen on the news that the FBI was hunting him, as if he were some common criminal, as if their role were to capture him. As if he weren't above their rules. The world *should* be a place where he could tell them to back off, and they would understand the necessity of it, but it didn't seem to work like that. Yet.

Kill someone here, on a crowded bus, and there would be consequences. It would complicate things unnecessarily. So he didn't. He stepped away instead, and stood further down the bus, watching and waiting, his gaze boring into the back of the young woman's skull.

He didn't get off at the stop he'd intended. Instead, he continued to wait, looking for his chance.

His moment would come, and then this disrespectful, *treasonous* woman would learn her place once and for all.

CHAPTER NINE

What did a realtor and a waitress at a Renaissance Faire have in common? What *could* they have in common, when it seemed that their lives were so different? That question was bugging Paige more now that their first suspect had an alibi for one of the murders, the frustration of that making her try to look for a connection.

It wasn't enough to find someone who had a potential reason to kill one victim, not when they were dealing with what appeared to be a serial killer. Paige needed to find something that fit for both of them, someone who had a reason to kill them both, and no alibi.

"I'll release Steve Baker," Christopher said. "Since he has an alibi for the first killing, we don't have enough to hold him."

Paige nodded. She'd known that was inevitable from the moment that he'd provided the alibi. In her mind, he'd almost faded away, leaving her to focus on things that might actually be relevant to catching the killer. The question now was where to look next.

Paige delved into what she could find of Meredith and Gisele's lives. She'd looked briefly on the flight over, but she wanted to be sure. Their social media accounts didn't suggest that they knew one another, but maybe there would be some other link.

Gisele had never visited the Renaissance Faire, as far as Paige could see, but with a place like that, it would be hard to tell. Maybe someone would announce their day out there on their social media pages, or maybe they would be too busy enjoying the atmosphere to do it. Not everyone announced every place they visited. Some people might even feel that posting about it didn't fit in with the general theme of the place, although from what Paige had seen, the Renaissance Faire seemed happy enough to embrace anachronisms.

Assume for a second that it wasn't there. Where else, then, might there be a connection? Paige found herself wondering if Meredith had used the services of a realtor in the last couple of months. If so, maybe there was a faint chance that the connection might lie somewhere there, and that the murders could all be traced back to that? People got pretty worked up about houses, so it was just about plausible that if someone had missed out on the home they wanted because of Meredith, then they might have been willing to kill her. And if Gisele were somehow connected to the deal too…

That hypothesis fell flat the moment that Paige saw that Meredith had lived in the same rented apartment for about three years. That was the problem with that kind of speculation: it could send her brain spiraling off down new paths, but unless the evidence was there to back it up, there was a risk of spending time and energy chasing shadows without making any real progress towards catching the killer.

Paige kept searching on her laptop, and as she did so, she caught sight of a news story just breaking, one she couldn't stop herself from clicking on.

Local Re-enactor Wrongly Arrested by FBI.

Paige knew that she shouldn't look, but in that moment, she couldn't hold back from reading it. She clicked on the story and quickly found herself looking at a video feed of Steve Baker standing outside the FBI field office. It seemed that the moment he'd been released, he'd decided to talk to the press who'd been waiting for any scrap that came their way.

"The FBI arrested me for no reason!" he declared to the cameras, injecting a note of hurt into his voice. "They startled my horse, and I was nearly killed when I fell off!"

"There's no point in watching that," Christopher said firmly, as he came back into the office. "It was inevitable from the moment we had to let Steve go. And of course the local press are primed to pick it all up."

Primed? Did that mean that someone, such as the local PD, had suggested to the press that they should wait for this?

"Do you think this is going to cause problems for us?" Paige asked. She could feel a dozen different worries building in her. What if Steve sued? What if the negative publicity made it harder for them to do their jobs here?

Christopher shook his head, though, casually, as if he'd been through it a dozen times before. Maybe he had.

"This is normal, particularly when the local police department isn't feeling cooperative. The press just want any story they can find to keep the news cycle going. Soon enough, they'll latch on to Steve Baker's record for stalking, and on the way he put people in danger while he tried to escape."

It was comforting hearing that, especially from Christopher, who knew what he was talking about in a way most others didn't. Paige felt

51

like she could trust that coming from him in a way that she might not have been able to from someone else. He was an experienced agent who had seen all of this before.

Maybe he also had some ideas about where to go next with all of this, now that their first lead had fallen through.

"I've been looking to try to find a connection between Meredith Park and Gisele Newbury," Paige said. "Some context in which the killer might have found them both, even if there's no obvious reason why they might have been killed."

"Did anyone make threats towards them?" Christopher asked. "Is there anything in their messages or emails to suggest someone who was building up to kill them, or who even just had a problem with them?"

That was a reasonable thought. After all, most people were killed by someone they knew, and it often wasn't a surprise. There was a pattern of behavior that built up to the moment of murder, escalating through arguments and often other forms of violence. Maybe that was true here. Maybe there would be a thread of messages to follow back to find the killer.

Paige looked, but she simply couldn't find anything like that in Meredith's messages. If anything, the interactions there only reinforced what people had said around the Renaissance Faire: that she was nice to everyone, and that everyone she met loved her. It was so wholesome that Paige actually found herself wondering if there might not be a nastier side to it all elsewhere, but she knew that was just the cynicism of someone who worked around death and violence all day. Meredith Park seemed to be genuinely well liked.

There was certainly no one there in her social media making threats against her, no one who looked as if they might be the killer.

"There's nothing here," Paige said. "At least not for Meredith. And if we find someone who was angry with Gisele, does that mean anything if there's no reason for them to kill both women?"

"It might," Christopher pointed out. "After all, Gisele was the first victim, and you've told me before that's more significant for a killer."

That was true. Often with serial killers, that first kill meant something particularly personal to them, had some kind of connection to their lives that their other kills didn't. Then, once they'd gotten a taste for it, some of them went on to kill strangers with no real connection to them or grievance against them, simply because they could.

Maybe that was what had happened here. Maybe the killer had murdered Gisele Newbury for a reason and realized that they liked killing so much that they'd then gone out to actively hunt another victim. And, if there were differences between the two, maybe that was because Gisele had been there in front of them because of the situation, while Meredith was a victim of choice.

Without more evidence, it was impossible to know for sure, but it was plausible. Certainly, it was a thought that suggested that Paige and Christopher should focus more on Gisele's death. In particular, Paige found herself wondering if the fleur-de-lis or the blade might have some significance within her life that would make them an integral part of the murders. Of course, Paige knew from her research so far that there was no sign of the fleur-de-lis on Gisele's social media, but maybe it would become relevant.

"Who would want to kill a realtor?" Paige said, trying to think of ways this might have happened.

"Someone feeling upset because of a property deal, maybe," Christopher replied. "There's a lot of money at stake with that kind of thing, and tempers can get pretty frayed. I can email her office and try to get details of anything she was working on at the time of her death. Then there will be lists of her potential clients. Maybe one of them will turn out to be upset enough with her to have potentially done this."

"Maybe," Paige said. "Although if we have to interview everyone on a realtor's client list one by one, it could take a lot of time, potentially with no reward, and in the meantime, the killer is still out there."

"Sometimes, grinding through the evidence is what it takes to catch someone," Christopher pointed out. Even he didn't sound like he wanted to risk leaving a killer out there like that, though. "But if we can find something that will lead us to him quicker, that would be better. It seems like Gisele is the key, though."

Paige nodded. It was just a question of working out how to make inroads without having to grind this down over days or even weeks. That would give the killer far too much time in which to kill again.

The circumstances of Gisele's death were odd, killed in her driveway, next to her car. Was that a deliberate ambush, or an indication of something else?

Paige found herself looking over the crime scene photographs. In particular, she looked at a wider shot of the scene, which showed Gisele's Porsche on the edge of the driveway, practically out in the road, like she'd stopped suddenly as soon as she was there, trying to get out of it and get inside. Like she was already afraid of something out there on the road.

But if she'd been in her car, what could she have been afraid of? There had been no one in there with her according to the forensics report; everything about the crime scene suggested that the killer had approached her once she was out of the car, then killed her with a single stab wound. That had happened when Gisele was already home. So what had her in such a rush to get out of her car and get to her front door, to try to get to safety?

Maybe a road rage incident? Or maybe the killer following her car? Either one of those might have inspired that kind of fear, and either way, there was a chance that something like that would have been reported.

Paige checked the location of Gisele's last viewing, then began to plot the route between there and her home. That gave her a sense of where Gisele would have been and when in the half hour before her death. Then she looked up the number for the local highway patrol. Hopefully, they would be more helpful than the rest of the Lexington PD had been so far, when it came to their investigations.

"Hello, how can I help you?" a woman's voice on the other end of the line said.

"Hi," Paige said. "This is Agent Paige King, with the FBI. I'm on the team investigating the murders of Gisele Newbury and Meredith Park."

She quickly provided her badge number for the highway patrol to check.

"Hello, Agent," the woman said. "What can I do for you?"

"I'm looking for any reports of erratic driving or road rage on a particular route between 4:30 and 5pm two days ago. Particularly anything involving a blue Porsche."

"If you send me the route and the license plate of the vehicle, then I can check," the woman said. "It will take me a minute to do it, though. I'll call you back."

Paige sent the information on Gisele Newbury's route over to the highway patrol's number, then waited. And waited. Was it possible that she wasn't going to get an answer? Maybe someone else at the highway patrol had pointed out to whoever had answered the phone that they weren't being helpful towards the FBI? If that proved to be the case, would she and Christopher have to go over there in person to try to get answers? Would they need to get a warrant for what they needed?

Then her phone rang, as the highway patrol called her back, and Paige snatched it up gratefully.

"Agent King?" the woman she'd spoken to before said. "We have a record of a call in that period, made by a Gisele Newbury. She reported that a car with no license plate was tailgating her, and flashing its lights aggressively. We dispatched a patrol car, but there was no sign of either Ms. Newbury or the other car by the time it got there."

Because Gisele Newbury had been running for home by that point, assuming that it would be the only place she might be safe. Only she hadn't made it home, because someone had killed her before she got inside her house. It had to be that driver who had followed her, didn't it?

Was this all about one road rage incident? Was that what had started this and cost two women their lives? Where did Meredith Park fit into it? Was she really just a random victim slain by a killer who had decided that he liked killing too much to stop?

It was possible. The strange wound shapes and the fleur-di-lis ornaments left at the scenes suggested that the two deaths were connected. It seemed too much to ask that someone had seen the news of Gisele's death and decided to copy the MO so precisely in such a short space of time. To source a small fleur-de-lis ornament like that would be hard enough, but the murder weapon would be almost impossible to copy, as Paige doubted that the shape of the dagger was a piece of information that had made it into the news.

No, this had to be one killer, didn't it? One who had started by killing Gisele after some petty road rage incident, and who had then moved on to kill another woman either because of some personal hatred or simply because he wanted to experience the thrill of killing someone again.

The connection could be that slight. If Gisele had been killed because of some traffic incident, then she was essentially a random victim, thrown into the killer's path. Meredith might potentially have meant more to him, or again, she might just have been in the wrong place at the wrong time, making her death essentially random.

"Agent King, are you still there?" the woman from the highway patrol agency asked, after a few seconds.

"Yes, sorry," Paige said.

"Did you need anything else?"

Did she? Was the confirmation of that call made by Gisele enough, or could Paige get more? It occurred to her that cars without license plates probably weren't that common around Lexington. That might make it possible to find what she was looking for.

"Am I right in thinking that traffic cameras would flag any cars without license plates automatically?" Paige asked.

"That's right."

Paige felt a note of hope rising in her.

"Then I need any traffic camera footage you have of vehicles on that route without a license plate between… let's say four and five."

"I'll see what I can do."

She hung up, leaving Paige to wait for the footage. She didn't know how many vehicles like that there were likely to be. Maybe it would mean she had to search through hours of clips, trying to find answers. It might not actually save any time, doing things this way. Paige hoped, though, that it might be just a few, and once she looked through the time stamps, she might be able to isolate the car that had been involved in the road rage incident with Gisele's Porsche.

From there, it would take some work, but Paige should be able to trace the vehicle back to its owner, and possibly to the man who had killed two women in two days.

CHAPTER TEN

When the traffic cam footage came through, Paige felt a wave of excitement, mixed in with the sudden awareness that she now needed to find a way to get something she could use from that footage. She had raw data, but now she needed to find a way to turn that into something useful.

She needed to work out which of these cars might be the one whose driver had been behaving aggressively towards Gisele Newbury, and from that, she needed to find a way to identify the driver. Two separate questions, but both leading towards the same end point.

There seemed to be three hits on the traffic cams for cars without license plates along the stretch of highway that Paige was interested in. Three was a small enough number to be manageable, letting Paige look through them, trying to pick out the correct one. Of those three, two had already been identified by the highway patrol. One belonged to a delivery vehicle, and Paige looked over to Christopher for help.

"Christopher, how hard would it be to trace the route of a delivery vehicle?"

"It shouldn't be hard. I'll call the company and ask them. You want to know if it went anywhere near Gisele Newbury's house or the Ren-Faire, right?"

Paige nodded. She was glad that Christopher understood what she was looking for with all of this, and that he was on the same wavelength when it came to investigating. She saw him lean over her shoulder to get the details of the van from the screen, and for an instant, that was far too close for Paige. She could feel her heart beating faster at his presence there and had to tell herself that she shouldn't be reacting to him like this.

"Ok, I've got it," Christopher said, moving away. "I'll try to get an answer from the delivery company one way or another."

Paige nodded her thanks, but that still left her with two vehicles to check. Paige turned to the next piece of footage, trying to see what it contained.

That section of footage had a pretty clear view of the car the traffic cameras had picked up: a minivan, and the footage gave Paige a good view through the windows of the vehicle. She saw a middle aged woman there, with five children of different ages, from what appeared to be a toddler all the way up to a teenager sitting in the passenger seat.

That left Paige with a simple question: did Paige really believe that this was the killer? It wasn't just that the majority of serial killers were male and younger, although that was a definite question mark against this being the car. No, Paige found herself wondering more about the simple practicality of the murder. Was she really saying that this woman had tailgated a Porsche in her minivan, followed Gisele Newbury home in it, and then killed her with five children watching?

It just didn't seem plausible that this could be the killer, even before throwing in the physical aspect of the two murders. This was a murderer who had approached from the front, overpowered his victims, and killed them with a single thrust of a knife. Paige just wasn't sure that the woman driving the minivan would have been able to do it. Then there was the question of the children. Had she really gone out and killed someone in front of what appeared to be her entire family?

"I've checked with the delivery company," Christopher said. "The delivery van didn't go anywhere near either murder site. I don't think that's the one we're looking for."

Especially not when the call to the highway patrol had talked about a *car* tailgating. That detail suggested that it wasn't either of the first two vehicles Paige had looked at, and *that* left only one vehicle for Paige to look at. Almost trembling in anticipation, she called up the footage on the third.

That footage looked far more promising to Paige's eye, showing a dark Dodge Charger that had obviously had custom work done to it, making its lines even more aggressive than they had started originally, its angles harsher. The windows were tinted, so there was no way to look through the windshield to see the driver, and the back license plate was missing. The whole thing seemed designed to intimidate anyone who looked.

That combination was going to make it harder to find the car's owner. Paige kept scrolling through the traffic cam footage, trying to find a moment when something more identifying might be visible. She *thought* she caught a glimpse of a front license plate, but it was so blurred that she couldn't pick out the details on the camera footage.

It was enough to bring a small sound of frustration from Paige, disappointed in the extreme at being able to make out the car but not having enough to identify it. Paige kept looking through the traffic cam footage, hoping that there would be a clearer shot of the vehicle that might show its license plate, but she couldn't see one. There didn't seem to be a single second when she could actually make out the numbers.

This was their current best suspect in Gisele Newbury's murder, and Paige couldn't identify him, whoever he was.

She needed a different camera angle, one that might give her a clearer shot of the car's front license plate, but there simply didn't appear to be what she needed in the traffic camera footage. Paige sat there staring at it, willing it to come into view, watching the car driving past a row of stores, trying to think of some way of getting the information she needed.

The answer hit her as she stared at the footage. Wouldn't those stores have security cameras of their own, to try to deter thieves? If just one of them had a camera facing onto the street, then Paige might be able to get what she needed.

"Do you think that we'll be able to get security footage from any of those stores?" Paige asked, pointing to several that the car was driving past.

Christopher nodded. "We can try."

*

As they stood on the sidewalk outside the row of stores that the Dodge had flashed past, Paige found her hopes dwindling a little. In the FBI field office, this had seemed easy, but here, the difficulties of it started to hit home. Was a store really going to hand over its security footage simply because the two of them asked? Were any of the stores even going to have a camera with an angle that might show the car? Would they even have access to their footage, if, like a lot of places, they stored it offsite?

Any of those difficulties might be the hurdle at which their attempt to catch the killer fell.

The first step was to find somewhere that might even have the footage that they needed. Thankfully, Christopher was already making his way along the row of stores, obviously checking them for cameras.

"This one has one, but it's facing the door," he said, quickly moving on to the next. "Nothing here. Ah, *here* we go."

He'd stopped in front of a brightly lit convenience store. It had a camera set just back from the door, obviously there to monitor anyone who set foot inside, but judging by the angle of it, the camera would also have a pretty good view of the street outside as well.

Paige and Christopher went in together, and now Paige felt a sense of determination rising in her. They needed to talk to the store owner, to try to get access to the camera footage.

The store owner was standing behind the broad expanse of a counter, a large man in his late thirties, wearing a grubby white shirt with the sleeves rolled up and dark slacks. He looked like he'd once been in good shape, but that had long since started to fade. His dark hair was cropped short and he gave the two of them a disapproving look as they approached.

"Do you two want to buy something?" he asked.

His tone wasn't friendly, and it took Paige a moment to realize exactly why. She and Christopher probably didn't look like his normal customers, and they'd just come into the store while staring at the cameras. To him, it must have looked like they were casing the store, trying to work out the best way to rob it without being caught.

"FBI," Christopher said, taking out his badge and placing it on the counter for the store owner to look at.

"You think I haven't seen a fake badge before?" The suspicion was still there. Maybe he thought that this was some kind of con, now.

Paige took out her own badge. "Look again. Call the local FBI field office to confirm who we are if you want. You've heard about the murders in the last couple of days? We're investigating them."

The store owner looked from her badge to Christopher's and back again, as if the sudden doubling of the numbers could persuade him of their authenticity.

"You don't think I had anything to do with all that?" the store owner said. He looked worried, as if he now thought that Paige and Christopher might be there to try to pin something on him. Or maybe had other secrets of his own that he didn't want them around for too long while they were here.

"No, sir," Christopher said. "But we think that you might be able to help us. Does your security camera at the front have a clear view of the street?"

The store owner shrugged. "I guess. Mostly I just use it to make sure kids aren't coming in to steal from me."

"Could we look at the footage?" Paige asked. "We think that a potential suspect may have driven by this store two days ago."

"I don't know." The store owner sounded like he didn't really want anything to do with any of this. "I don't want to get involved. I don't want to have to be a witness or anything."

"You wouldn't be involved," Paige said. "We just need the footage, that's all. And just letting us do that might be enough to help us catch a murderer."

Paige could still see the indecision on the features of the store owner, and she found herself wondering if she and Christopher were going to have to come back here with a warrant. If they could even get one for this. Yet she didn't say anything, didn't want to put any more pressure on the store owner than he was under already.

"All right," he said. "Come on back to the office."

He led the way back to a grimy office that was halfway to being a storeroom, there were so many boxes stacked up in it. There was a computer there, and the store owner typed in a password, then clicked on a few icons, calling up his security feed.

"There," he said, gesturing for Paige to take over. "It's all yours. I have to get back to serving customers."

There weren't any customers in the store that Paige could see through the doorway to the office, but she was grateful to be left in charge of the security footage.

"Can you find the right time?" Christopher asked.

Paige nodded. "I know what time the car was passing the store from the traffic cameras. So if I just find the same time on this…"

She scrolled back, looking for that moment. Paige got to with a couple of minutes of it quickly, and then watched forward in real time. She had to look beyond the door to the convenience store, trying to take in what was happening on the street. As cars flashed by outside, Paige watched for the one she wanted.

She saw what looked like the right one, rewound, and then watched again, moving forward frame by frame.

"There!" Christopher said. "There's a clear shot of the license plate there."

Paige froze the footage, staring at the still image. As Christopher had said, the freezeframe showed the Dodge outside the store, and the angle was far better than the traffic camera, giving Paige a clear view of its license plate.

"Is that a five?" she asked, trying to make out the full plate.

"I think it might be a three," Christopher said.

Now that he'd said it, Paige could see that it was. She took the number and ran it through the DMV. She then took the name and put it into the FBI's systems to see what came up.

"Nick Lloyd," Paige said. "A local veterinarian. He has priors for a couple of bar fights."

"A man with a temper, then?" Christopher said. "Someone with low impulse control, at least."

Paige nodded, downloading the footage onto her laptop for future reference. That was intriguing. A man who was prone to lashing out potentially fit the profile that was starting to form in her mind. It certainly fit with the idea of someone who had killed Gisele Newbury as a result of some kind of bout of road rage.

What was even more intriguing was his address. When Paige looked it up on a map, the location sent immediate red flags flashing in her.

"He only lives about a mile from the Renaissance Faire," Paige said. Close enough that he could easily have been there. Close enough that if he wanted to hunt for someone else to kill, then that would be an easy place for him to seek out a victim."

"I think we need to talk to Nick Lloyd."

CHAPTER ELEVEN

It was getting into evening as Paige and Christopher approached Nick Lloyd's place, the light starting to fade around them. It was a large house on the fringes of Lexington, modern, boxy, and expensive looking, with the lawn neatly trimmed and the paint gleaming in the sun as if it had been freshly repainted. As they pulled up, Paige could just about see the Ren-Faire in the distance over open ground beyond the house. Close enough that it would have been easy for Nick Lloyd to slip into it unseen. Close enough that it might have been the obvious place for him to try to find victims.

More of her immediate attention was on the car in the driveway. It was a black Dodge Charger, and this close, Paige could see the custom work done to it, the same custom work that had been there in the traffic camera footage. Good, that meant that even if the convenience store owner didn't want them using him as a witness in court, they would be able to prove that this was the car that had been harassing Gisele Newbury just before her death. There was still no back license plate, but Paige had no doubt that the front one would match. They were in the right place.

She and Christopher pulled up alongside the Charger, and Paige could feel the tension building in both of them. They'd found the right spot, and it was obvious that their suspect was home. Now, they just needed to see how Nick Lloyd would react to being accused of murder.

"Be ready," Christopher said, with a worried note in his voice. "If this is our killer, then he's already proved that he's capable of overpowering people quickly, and he doesn't hesitate to kill."

"I don't think he'll find us quite as easy to take down," Paige said. She'd fought and arrested dangerous killers before. She'd had far more training than either of this killer's victims. She was determined not to be dead weight in this partnership. She would do her part in taking Nick Lloyd down, if necessary.

Still, she wasn't going to underestimate him. Not when he'd already shown how deadly he could be with a knife. This was potentially a very dangerous man. Paige got out of the car, her hand going automatically to check the Glock 19 that sat at her waist. She wanted to be able to draw it cleanly if she needed it. Christopher was out of the car too, slowly approaching the door to the house.

They crept forward, moving carefully. Paige could feel the tension rising.

"Down!" Christopher yelled, and even though Paige couldn't see the reason for it, she ducked.

An instant later, there was a boom that Paige recognized from her hours on the FBI range as a shotgun. She saw the front passenger side tire on their car blow out as the shotgun blast hit it.

Paige reacted on instinct and scrambled back to the car, using it for cover as she drew her weapon and looked around for the potential threat. Paige could feel her training coming back to her, the endless drills at the academy making her react automatically. Christopher was there too, staying low.

"FBI!" he called out, obviously assuming that this was some kind of case of mistaken identity that might be resolved just by identifying themselves. "Throw down your weapon and come out with your hands up!"

Another shotgun blast was the only answer to that, going wide this time, but still making Paige flinch. She fired back in the direction the blast had come from, but there was no sign that she hit anything with her shot.

Paige could see the Dodge Charger next to her, and now that she was out of the car, huddled down next to it, she could hear its engine running, too. Its driver's side door was open, and Paige could see the keys there in the ignition. It looked as though Nick was getting ready for a quick getaway.

That only raised Paige's suspicions. Who but the killer would want to make a run for it like that, and would react so violently when the FBI showed up?

"We're pinned down," Christopher said, as the shotgun continued to blare. "I can't pop up to get a clean shot, because it's too exposed."

Paige leaned out momentarily, trying to find an opportunity to get off a clean shot of her own, but she had to quickly duck back behind the car as another shower of lead shot came her way. She fired off another shot blind, just to keep their assailant at bay, but it didn't seem to slow down the attack. More shotgun blasts came, pinning her down, making it impossible to move out to try to take their suspect down.

She and Christopher couldn't stay there, but they were also stuck in place behind the car, sitting ducks for the shotgun if they tried to move. Paige had an idea, though.

"Come on," she said to Christopher, and made a run for the Charger's open door. Another shotgun blast came, missing her by what felt like just inches, the lead shot whispering past her, but Paige kept her head down and threw herself into the car in one movement, with Christopher following just a moment or two later.

"What's your plan?" he asked, as he ducked down behind the dash.

"If Nick there is planning a quick getaway, I figure taking his getaway vehicle is probably a good first step," Paige said. "Plus, this gets us out of his line of fire and lets us regroup."

She threw the car into gear, then reversed down the driveway while more shotgun blasts followed them. Paige ducked as one shattered the rear window, feeling a rush of fear at the possibility that the next blast might hit her or Christopher, the blast showing just how vulnerable they were like that, but she kept driving, speeding away down the lane that led to Nick's house.

Paige drove for a minute or more before she pulled up a little way away, abandoning the car.

"Ok, we're clear," she said, looking around. There was no sign that Nick was following with his shotgun.

"Are you hurt?" Christopher asked, taking hold of her arms, and looking her over. He looked worried by the prospect, his eyes searching Paige frantically for any sign of injury.

"I'm fine," Paige assured him. It was a strange feeling, having Christopher pay her such close attention, even if it was just to check that she wasn't injured.

"Are you sure? Sometimes, with gunshots, it can take a minute to sink in."

"No, I'm fine." Paige had been terrified when some of the shotgun blasts had come too close to her, but none of them had touched her. At least, she didn't think they had. She'd been lucky. They both had. That could have gone a lot worse. It would only have taken one of those shotgun blasts to be on target, and they would be dead. "Are you ok?"

"I'm fine, but we can't just leave like this," Christopher said. "We've just moved away from a scene where we have a shooter we suspect of being a serial killer. He still has the weapon, and now he knows the FBI is looking for him. We have to contain that situation."

"We will," Paige said. "But we couldn't do anything while he had us pinned down like that."

They'd needed to get clear to have any chance of approaching the situation from a new angle.

"We need to get back there," Christopher said. Paige could see him assessing the situation. "But not the front way. He could still be watching for us. We'll go around back and try to catch him by surprise."

Paige was impressed by how quickly Christopher was ready to go back and face an armed man again, and how quickly he'd come up with a plan to do it, but then, that was their job. They had to be ready to take on the people no one else would, to make sure that the public was safe from the most dangerous people out there.

"Should we call for backup?" Paige asked.

"The Lexington PD hasn't been helpful so far, and I'm not sure there's time," Christopher said. "By the time they get here, Nick could have escaped. We need to act now."

He had a point. If Nick was their killer, and he was running around with a shotgun, there was no telling how much damage he might do now that he knew the FBI were looking for him. He might abandon his usual choice of weapon and just go on a spree, determined to kill as many as possible before he was caught.

Christopher started to run with a long loping stride and Paige had to hurry to keep up with him. She was determined too, wanting to make sure that Nick Lloyd didn't have the chance to hurt anyone. She'd had to run in her training; there had been minimum times to hit just to make the grade to be an agent. That training stood Paige in good stead now, letting her keep up in spite of her much shorter legs and smaller frame. She just about managed to keep up with Christopher, heading down a passage into the backyard of one of Nick's neighbors.

Now, it was like being on one of the obstacle courses back at Quantico, throwing herself over garden fences, trying not to slow down while she did it. It was important to keep up momentum, her instructors had told her, because stopping in front of each obstacle was a surefire way to lose a suspect in a chase. Here, Paige wasn't pursuing a fleeing perpetrator, but every moment she and Christopher took in getting back to the house was one that Nick Lloyd might use to try to escape or hurt someone else.

Paige threw herself over another high fence, and now she found herself in a yard with a large dog. That dog stared at her, growled, and then barked a warning. Christopher was already halfway across that yard, and Paige saw him clamber up a chain link fence on the other side. Paige still had to cover the ground, and the dog's eyes seemed to be focusing on her as it continued to growl.

Paige backed slowly towards the fence now, not wanting to do anything that might startle the animal into attacking. She was aware of the presence of her gun in her hand, but the last thing Paige wanted to do right then was to shoot someone's dog just because it was trying to protect their yard.

The dog growled again then, starting towards her, and Paige ran the few remaining strides to the fence on pure fear. She leaped at it and knew halfway through that it wasn't going to be enough to make it to the top. She was going to be stuck there, and the dog would attack, and…

Christopher's arm reached down, grabbing her wrist in a vicelike grip. He pulled Paige up, showing no sign of effort at hauling her smaller form up the fence, letting her clamber over it and drop to the other side, panting in the aftermath of her fear.

"Are you ok?" he asked, taking a moment to crouch in front of her.

Paige made herself nod. They had a suspect to catch, and no time to waste on making sure that she was fine. "We need to keep going."

Paige kept moving, running again to keep up with Christopher. Now, they were approaching Nick Lloyd's property, getting close to the wooden fence that surrounded it. They started to slow down, because they couldn't afford to attract attention when Nick had already shown how willing he was to open fire if he saw them. They had to approach without being seen or heard now. Paige kept low, moving along the fence line, watching out for danger.

She saw Christopher look over the fence, checking for danger and a way in. "We can go over here. He's not in the yard."

He led the way, and Paige vaulted over the fence after him smoothly, landing in a neatly kept yard that had a couple of apple trees at one end. Paige swept it for the possibility of danger automatically, keeping her Glock close to her body, ready to come up to meet any threat. Paige kept her eyes on the house, a couple of large French windows letting her see into a dining room beyond. Paige couldn't see any signs of movement from inside the house, but she padded towards it anyway, not wanting to risk attracting attention when the two of them were still out in the open.

Paige saw a passage leading to the front of the property and started down it, still moving quietly. From that passage, she could see a man who had to be Nick Lloyd standing there in front of the house, examining Paige and Christopher's car. It was Paige's first good look at him. He was a large man, heavily built and square jawed, holding a shotgun in one meaty hand while the other was on the roof of the car.

"Bastards, when I catch up to them, I'll kill them for taking my car and my stuff!"

He sounded as though he meant the threat in that moment, especially when he'd already shot at them once. He certainly looked angry enough, red faced and moving erratically. Was it this anger that had cost Gisele and Meredith their lives? Had they found the killer they were looking for?

Paige could worry about that once they had Nick in custody. Whatever else he might or might not have done, he'd fired at Paige and Christopher even after they'd identified themselves as FBI. He'd gone out of his way to try to kill them both. He needed to be stopped, and stopped now, before his obvious anger could hurt anyone else. They had to move in and take him down cleanly.

Paige looked over at Christopher, who gestured to one side of their suspect, then to himself, then to the other. Paige nodded as she understood the simple plan he was proposing. He wanted the two of them to flank him, and take him from either side, so that he wouldn't have a chance to fight back against them both. He was dangerous when he was able to fire at them from cover, but when they both had their weapons trained on him, would he be as tough?

Paige edged forward, swinging wide around him, while Christopher moved in the other direction, so that they could approach Nick Lloyd from either side. Paige made sure that she was never directly opposite Christopher, though, because she didn't want him in her line of fire if things went bad.

Paige moved as quietly as she could. Even so, she was just a couple of paces from Nick when he turned, and she realized that he obviously intended to go back into the house. Paige saw the look of shock on his face, quickly replaced by anger and determination as he started to raise the weapon he held.

Paige reacted on instinct, moving in closer to him before he could bring it to bear. She hooked her leg behind his, tripping him, sending them both tumbling to the ground. Paige managed to get both of her hands on the shotgun, wrenching it away from the bigger man with all her might. She wasn't as strong, but he couldn't deal with her whole body weight against his grip. She felt the moment when Nick lost his grip on the weapon and Paige kicked it away from the two of them.

Christopher was there then, his gun leveled at Nick Lloyd, his weight joining Paige's in pinning him down.

"Don't move, Lloyd," he said. "Don't even think about it. You've already fired at us, so don't think for a moment that I'll hesitate."

For a moment, Paige thought that their suspect might try to wrench free, because she could see the anger on his face. Slowly, though, in the face of a weapon trained on him, that anger started to give way to a kind of resignation. Paige got out her handcuffs, taking his arms and cuffing them behind him to restrain him.

"Nick Lloyd, you're under arrest."

CHAPTER TWELVE

Paige waited outside the interrogation room of the FBI field office while Nick Lloyd conferred with his lawyer, working out how he was going to deal with the trouble he was currently in. He sat there, perfectly poised, as if he hadn't just fired at Paige and Christopher repeatedly, hadn't tried to kill them both in an effort to keep from being arrested.

"Why does he look so confident?" Christopher asked. He sounded slightly worried, obviously not used to suspects reacting like this.

"It could just be a bluff," Paige said. "Some people try to project that they've done nothing wrong, and they have nothing to worry about. But it could be something else."

Christopher frowned at that. "Such as?"

"Our killer is likely to be a psychopath, so he might not feel this moment the same way someone else might. And you saw the photographs of the scenes. This is a very controlled killer. He lashes out, but he does it in a precise way, a controlled way."

"Either way, I think we need to get in there," Christopher said.

Paige could only agree. The two of them headed into the interrogation room, taking seats on the strangely plush furniture near Nick and his lawyer. Nick Lloyd's lawyer was a thirty-something man with slicked-back dark hair and an expression of mild disdain for the FBI.

He went on the attack almost as soon as Paige and Christopher entered the room, barely giving them a chance to sit down.

"My client has been wrongfully arrested. The two of you burst onto his property without a warrant, and when he attempted to defend himself, you stole his car, sneaked back onto his property, and assaulted him. We will be demanding a public apology from the FBI, and I require that you let Mr. Lloyd go at once."

He was obviously hoping that sheer pressure would convince them to let Nick Lloyd go. Except… would any competent lawyer really think that? No, Paige realized, he was just trying to rattle them and put them on the back foot. He wanted to take control of this interrogation, presumably to limit his client's chances of incriminating himself. That

70

suggested that there was something there he didn't want Paige and Christopher to find out.

"That's not going to happen," Christopher said. "Agent King and I clearly identified ourselves as federal agents. Mr. Lloyd continued to fire on us after we did so. He also shot at us the moment we pulled up. We hadn't shown any aggressive intent."

"Do you have any proof of that?" the lawyer asked, with another contemptuous expression that said he didn't believe it for a minute.

Did they? Was this really going to be just their word against that of their suspect? Christopher didn't seem fazed by the question, though. In fact, he seemed like he'd been expecting it.

"The vehicle we arrived in was borrowed from this field office. It has cameras that recorded the entire incident. The audio from those will prove exactly what I just said. I'm sure you'll argue over it in court, but we currently have your client on charges of attempting to kill two federal agents."

Paige thought that she could detect the slightest note of tension in the lawyer's features.

"I'd like to see that footage."

"The vehicle is being recovered from Mr. Lloyd's house as we speak."

"Then you currently don't have anything."

Paige sighed. She suspected that the lawyer and Christopher might keep going around and around like this all day if nothing changed, when there were crucial questions that still needed to be asked about the case that had brought them to Nick's house in the first place.

"The Dodge Charger on your driveway is your car, right, Nick?" she asked.

He gave her an angry look. "Yes, it's mine. You bastards stole it."

"You seem like a very angry man, Nick," Paige said, not rising to meet that aggression. "Does that anger ever spill over into road rage? Driving too close to people? Flashing your lights? Trying to scare them?"

"You're jumping from accusations of assaulting the two of you to whether my client hit his horn because someone cut him off at a junction?" the lawyer asked, sounding incredulous at the question.

Paige nodded. "It's relevant. How about it, Nick? Do you ever get like that when you drive?"

"Sure, who doesn't?" Nick countered, making it sound as though it was normal.

71

"And did you have a road rage incident like that two days ago involving this woman?"

Paige pulled up an image of Gisele Newbury on her phone, showing it to Nick. He might not even know her name, but he would remember her if he'd argued with her. If he'd killed her.

"Did you argue with her? Did you follow her home?"

"I didn't even see her," Nick said. "It wasn't me."

"Really?" Paige said. "She was driving a Porsche, going about her day…"

"She was driving like a maniac!" Nick said, in a sudden burst of temper.

Paige looked over to Christopher, who nodded. He'd caught that slip too. It was kind of hard not to when Nick had reacted so obviously.

"I thought you said you've never seen her?" Christopher said. "If you haven't seen her, how do you know she was driving like a maniac?"

Nick engaged in a quick, whispered conversation with the lawyer.

"All right," he admitted once it became clear that the lawyer wasn't going to be able to do anything. "I saw her. I got pissed with her because she was driving that Porsche of hers insanely, all over the road. So yeah, I flashed my lights and tailgated her a little. So what?"

"So, the woman in question, Gisele Newbury, is dead," Paige said. She watched Nick, trying to gauge any hint of reaction to that. There wasn't any sign of sympathy now, or shock, only worry. Worry that he was about to be caught for his crimes? Worry that they'd found out what he'd done?

"I never had anything to do with that," Nick said, in a firm tone.

"So you didn't follow her home after your bout of road rage, then stab her?" Christopher asked.

Now Paige saw Nick's eyes widen, the accusation obviously taking him by surprise.

"No, of course not."

It would have been too much to hope that he might admit it. Of course he was going to deny it. It fell to her and Christopher to get past that denial to the truth.

"You just said that she made you angry," Paige said, seeing if that would get the reaction that they needed. "And we've seen that you're willing to lash out with violence."

"But not like that!" Nick said. "When you came to my house, I thought…"

72

"What did you think?" Christopher asked. "That you'd been caught? That we'd found out about Gisele, and about Meredith Park?"

"Who?" Nick said, but it wasn't very convincing. The idea that he wouldn't have at least heard the news of her death when it happened only around a mile from his home just wasn't believable.

Paige decided to press him on that aspect, hoping that if she kept switching angles, he would let something slip.

"Have you ever been to the Renaissance Faire?" Paige asked him.

He frowned, as if not quite sure where she was going with it. "Sure, I've been there. It's more for geeks and kids, but it's fun enough if I'm bored."

Paige called up a photograph of Meredith. "While you were there, did you see this woman?"

Nick shook his head, although it was hard to tell if he even really looked at the picture. "I've never seen her before."

"The same way you never saw Gisele Newbury before?" Christopher asked.

Nick's lawyer stepped in then. "My client has answered your question, Agent. If you don't have anything more relevant, I suggest that you let him go."

The lawyer was still angling for that? As far as Paige could see, that wasn't going to happen, but the lawyer was still pushing for it, almost with a hint of desperation. It was as if he thought that the longer Nick was here, the more chance there was of Paige and Christopher finding out something else.

What, though? What were the two of them trying to hide?

Paige found herself thinking back to the moment when she'd been sneaking up on Nick, and he'd been talking about killing her and Christopher for taking his car. That hadn't been the whole reason, though. He'd been upset that they'd taken his "stuff."

"What do you have in your car, Nick?" Paige asked, keeping her voice level.

She saw his eyes widen with fear at that, and knew that she'd hit close to home with the question.

"I don't know what you're talking about." It was a rote denial, and Paige didn't believe it.

"Sure you do. Now, we *could* have a team of FBI forensic experts tear the Dodge apart piece by piece until they find something, or you could give me an answer."

73

Was it the murder weapon? Was that what he was hiding? They were going to have to search the car carefully in any case, although Paige wasn't sure if their budget currently ran to the kind of effort that was going to take a forensic team for something like that.

"Nick," Christopher said. "If you make us search, then whatever we find, it won't go easy for you. If we find anything that could have been used in the murders…"

"I never murdered anyone!" Nick shouted, losing his cool, his temper on full display. "I'm a horse doper, not a killer!"

"A horse doper?" Paige asked. That took her a little by surprise.

Nick looked over to his lawyer, who clearly wanted to try to salvage the situation after his client's outburst.

"Before my client goes on, I want guarantees that information he provides will be taken into consideration by any court."

"Right now, he still has to convince us that he isn't a killer," Christopher said, not giving any ground. "If he provides information that's useful in other investigations, that will be noted, but this is *not* the moment to start angling for some kind of deal."

There was a note of authority there that seemed to take the lawyer aback. Paige had seen Christopher in this kind of commanding mode before, and she had to admit that it was always impressive. It made it harder to remember for a second or two that she wasn't meant to be attracted to him.

"How am I meant to prove I'm not a killer?" Nick said, his voice suddenly wheedling.

Paige had at least part of the answer to that. "How about if you start by telling us where you went after you followed Gisele Newbury down the street?"

"I went home," Nick said.

"Alone?" Paige asked. "Can anyone confirm that you were there?"

"Well… no."

He was looking pretty scared by now, as if he was only just starting to realize exactly how much trouble he was in, and that he might actually find himself charged with the murders.

"What about yesterday?" Paige asked. "Where were you around 5pm? Were you anywhere near the Renaissance Faire?"

Now he looked more relieved, although only slightly. "No, I wasn't. I wasn't even in Lexington."

"Where were you then?" Christopher asked.

"I…"

"If you don't provide us with details, why should we believe you, Nick?" Paige asked. She wasn't just going to take his word for it, after all.

"I was at a racetrack, working," Nick said.

"And by 'working' you mean that you were doping horses?" Christopher asked.

Nick nodded. "There was a favorite that needed to be slowed down enough for my clients to make a profit."

"And can anyone confirm that you were at the racetrack?" Christopher asked. That might be hard when he'd been trying to work without being seen.

"I went in through the turnstiles, same as everyone else. There will be cameras, right? Or people will remember me."

Meaning that if Paige and Christopher put in the work to chase this alibi, they would probably find that Nick Lloyd couldn't have been Meredith Park's killer. Paige felt disappointment spreading through her at that thought. She'd been so confident once Nick started shooting at her and Christopher that he was their man, but now, it seemed that they were back to the beginning on all of this. They would have to check, but she knew what they would find: Nick Lloyd, at a local racetrack, with a perfect alibi for Meredith's death.

Christopher stood up, gesturing for Paige to come with him outside. Paige went, the two of them leaving Nick and his lawyer back in the interrogation room.

"It's not him, is it?" Paige said.

Christopher shook his head. "It's possible that the alibi is fake but... I don't think so. We'll charge him anyway, for shooting at us, and for his 'work,' but I don't think this is our guy. We need to find someone else."

The knowledge that they weren't any closer to finding an answer even after being shot at was like a punch to the gut for Paige. It was frustrating, devastating, to know that they still didn't have answers after they'd put in so much work and been put in so much danger.

Paige was still fuming at it when Christopher's phone went off.

"Agent Marriott."

He stood there for several seconds, listening. Just the expression on his face told Paige that it wasn't anything good.

"I understand," he said at last. "We'll be right there."

"What is it?" Paige asked as Christopher hung up. His expression said that it was too much to hope that it had been a lead, and they were going to follow up on it.

"We have another reason now to think that Nick isn't the killer," Christopher said.

"Why?"

"Because there has been another murder while he was in our custody."

CHAPTER THIRTEEN

He walked through Lexington's main bus depot, away from the site of his most recent duel with one of those who had insulted him. The woman who had dared to wrong him lay dead, slain by his skill with a blade, justice done for her insult at last. Not that things could have turned out any other way. It wasn't as if any lesser person could hope to match him.

His blade was back in place beneath his suit, carefully strapped to the small of his back, where it belonged. Close enough to touch, close enough to pull out at any point when he needed it. There was a sense of power that came from having it there, although he liked to think that the power was within him anyway. The blade was merely an expression of that power, and of that status, a way of showing it to those who refused to recognize it the easy way.

He walked back to the ranks of waiting taxis, and selected his coach from among those lined up to serve, getting in and sitting there behind the driver. The engine of the modern conveyance was running, the driver's hands upon the wheel.

The driver barely glanced back at him.

"Where to?" he asked, in a gruff tone.

That summoned his ire a little. A servant such as this should be more deferential, should recognize the obvious difference between the two of them simply from his bearing and respond accordingly.

"Where to, *sire*," he said.

The driver looked around with a flash of something that might have been confusion, or might have been annoyance. Then it looked like he might say something impolite back, and *that* sent his hand questing for the spot where his weapon lay. He wasn't about to tolerate such a thing, even so soon after he had administered justice to another.

Then the driver seemed to swallow back whatever annoyance he felt.

"Where to, sir?"

Sir, not sire, but it was close enough.

"Just drive," he said. "I'll give you directions from there."

"Drive?" the driver said, as if he didn't understand the concept. Was he stupid? It was hard to make allowances for the foolish, even though almost everyone was, compared to him.

"Just do it, if you want to keep your job," he snapped. He could take away everything from this man, up to and including his life, but that threat seemed like enough for now.

"It's your money... sir," the driver said.

The driver started to drive, moving off smoothly, leaving behind the spot where he'd made his last kill. The woman from the bus lay dead, her eyes wide and staring in shock, as if she hadn't expected rightful retribution for her disrespect.

Already, he could feel the urge to duel someone else and show them their place, to end the life of someone else who didn't treat him with the respect that he was due. He'd thought that he would grow tired of killing mere peasants soon enough, but he found that he felt stronger the more of them he killed. Each one he slew was a testament to his power and importance. He was the one who survived their encounters, so he was automatically superior. Each death he inflicted was proof that he was the one with the power over life and death.

Killing didn't give him power, but it *proved* his power, over and over. It made him feel alive, made him feel like the only person in the world who mattered. He *was* the only person who mattered, others out there only to serve him or to be slain by him for their errors. They went about their petty lives, but he had an impact on the world.

He knew then that he would have to kill again soon, but that was all right, because he already had plenty of ideas about exactly who he would kill next.

CHAPTER FOURTEEN

Paige was surprised to find herself and Christopher heading to a busy bus terminal. This was where a murder had taken place? It seemed improbable, like it didn't quite fit with the pattern of the killings. The previous two had been in the open air, near vehicles, in spots where there hadn't been many people around. This seemed to Paige like the complete opposite of all three of those things. It was a public place, featuring buses rather than cars, and it was indoors.

Was her profile of the killer wrong? Was there even anything to connect this crime to the others? Presumably there had to be or the Lexington PD wouldn't have called them in. It was obvious that the local police department didn't want them there in the town, so they would only call Paige and Christopher in if they were sure that they had no choice about it.

It would be easy to tell, too, thanks to the fleur-de-lis.

The bus depot was thronging with people, ready to head out wherever they were going. The fact of the murder didn't seem to have gotten out yet, or if it had, it wasn't stopping people from going about their days normally. Buses still stood in waiting rows underneath a broad, arching roof, and people lined up in front of them to get aboard. Paige couldn't even make out any waiting press yet, which suggested that she and Christopher had gotten there early, before the news had a chance to get out. Paige doubted that would last.

Christopher flashed his badge to one of the depot's security personnel as he and Paige entered the place.

"FBI," he said.

The security guard looked relieved. "Thank God you're here. The local PD have left us guarding the scene but they've all gone. The moment they saw that strange ornament thing, they just said that it was the FBI's problem, not theirs."

Paige could hardly believe that they'd abandoned a crime scene to a few security guards so casually. Was the local PD really being so petty that it would just abandon a crime scene before the FBI even arrived? Did they really hope that Paige and Christopher would fail that badly? She just hoped that the security guards at the bus station had been able to preserve the scene enough that there was still a chance of collecting evidence.

Then again, at the initial two scenes, there hadn't been much to find in the first place. The forensic reports had suggested that the speed of the attacks and the clean kills had left little in the way of physical evidence. Maybe it would be different, though, indoors.

"Show us to the crime scene," Christopher said, obviously wanting to take control of the situation.

The security guard nodded and led the way through the station. Now, it seemed to Paige that people were watching, as if they knew that she and Christopher were FBI, and that something must be going on. Maybe people had seen them on the news and knew that they were linked to this case. Maybe just their presence there advertised that this was another kill for the serial killer, and would quickly bring the press running. Paige imagined that by the time she and Christopher were done, the press would be there, trying to find out what was going on.

That thought worried Paige. It meant that she and Christopher might not have much time before they also had to fend off questions from reporters while they tried to do their jobs. She quickened her stride behind the security guard.

The guard led the way to a set of locker rooms. Those were closed off with police tape, and another guard stood at the entrance. Through the door, Paige could see a team that had to be from the coroner's office, working to move a body into a body bag. At least they were still there, although there didn't seem to be any sign of a forensics team working with them on the crime scene.

Christopher seemed to have the same thought. "I'll make a call, see if I can get an FBI forensics team to sweep the place."

"Won't there be a lot of random people going through there?" Paige asked. With a bus station, there might be so many people going in and out of a locker room that it would be simply impossible to use forensics to pick one out as the potential killer.

"At least they can try to get fingerprints and DNA off the fleur-de-lis the local PD found," Christopher said. "And we can at least try to place anyone we do find at the scene."

He had a point, but it also meant that it wasn't going to give them what they needed to find their killer. All they were going to be able to manage, at best, was to confirm who the killer was once they'd caught him. To Paige, it didn't feel like enough, when they seemed to have so little to go on at the moment.

She ducked under the police tape and went inside with Christopher. The locker room was large and broadly square, but divided up by a couple of blocks of lockers that stood like islands at intervals in the middle of the room. It probably let the bus station fit more lockers in there, but it would also have meant that the killer had a chance to sneak up on his victim without any chance of being seen.

As far as Paige could tell, the coroner's people were just finishing up. A body bag lay closed on a gurney, ready to be wheeled out, while a quartet of techs stood there, waiting for the go ahead to take the victim away. One figure in a blue plastic evidence suit approached them as they entered the locker room. He was a man in his fifties, with a salt and pepper beard and blue eyes. He looked Paige and Christopher up and down as they approached.

"Are you the FBI?" he asked.

Paige nodded, showing her badge.

"I'm Jim Hough, the coroner. I can't say I approve of leaving a crime scene unattended like this, but that's between you and the local police department, I guess."

Paige found herself thinking that this whole business would be a lot easier if the local police were inclined to cooperate, but they still seemed to be playing the game of standing back and waiting for the FBI to falter, so that they could step in and claim the credit. In the meantime, people were dying, and that only made it more imperative that she and Christopher catch the killer. It seemed obvious now that he wasn't going to slow down or stop until they found him.

"Can you tell us anything about the victim?" Christopher asked.

"Her ID says that she's Peggy Cane. She has a college ID that suggests she's a local art major," the coroner said. He handed over a plastic evidence bag with a driver's license in it. Its photograph showed a spike-headed young woman in her early 20s. She was pretty but there was a hard edge to that prettiness that suggested she didn't take nonsense from anyone.

She didn't look anything like Meredith Park or Gisele Newbury, and if she was a student, then there was no initial reason to think that there would be a link between her life and those of the others either. Paige just had to hope that there would be something about this scene that would put her and Christopher on the right track.

"What's your initial assessment of the cause of death?" Christopher asked.

"A single stab wound to the heart. I can't tell you about the blade profile yet, because that will need to wait for my autopsy, but we did find this near the body."

He lifted another evidence bag. It held another of those small iron fleur-de-lis ornaments that had been there next to the first two victims. That seemed to make it clear that it was the same killer. The only question now was if there was anything about this location that might make it possible to actually find the killer.

"There will be plenty of security cameras here in the station, right?" Paige asked Christopher.

He nodded. "Here, and on the buses. If we can identify which one Peggy was on, there might be a chance to spot the moment when the killer selects her as a target."

It was probably their best chance for now. Paige went back to the edge of the scene, looking for the security guard who had brought them there. He was still standing just outside, as if waiting to see if there was anything else he could do that might help to resolve all of this. She was glad that he was eager to help, even if the local PD weren't.

"Can you get us access to the security footage for the station?" she asked.

The guard nodded. "We thought you might want that, so we've pulled up what we have in the security room. Just follow me."

He led the way through the station again, and now Paige saw that the press had started to gather, standing around with their cameras pointed her way. They started to call out questions as she passed.

"Agent King! Can you tell us what's going on here?"

"We're not releasing information at this time," she said, reflecting for a moment that she was starting to sound like a real FBI agent now, with that deadpan tone that didn't give anything away about the details of the investigation.

"What do you say to the accusation that the FBI isn't making progress? That you've already arrested the wrong man once, and it's costing people their lives?"

Paige flinched at those words because they hit far too close to home. The truth was that they hadn't found answers so far, and their attempts to do so had only taken them in the wrong direction. Because of that, another woman lay dead, stabbed by a psychopath. Could the local PD have done a better job in so short a time? Paige doubted it, but it still hurt to think about.

"We are continuing to work hard to catch the killer," Christopher said. "In spite of the Lexington PD providing no assistance."

It wasn't like him to say something like that, much less to say it and walk off, as he did now. Paige hurried to catch up with him.

"What was that?" Paige asked him.

"The press got here too fast for it to be a member of the public telling them that we were here," Christopher said. "Which means the local cops must have tipped them off, trying to make us look bad. I can deal with them not helping, but I won't put up with them playing games like this."

"You don't think that there will be any comebacks for a comment like that?" Paige asked.

She saw Christopher shrug, as if it didn't matter. "I'll deal with it."

"No, *we'll* deal with it," Paige corrected him. They were a team, after all.

For now, though, there was still the question of the security footage for the bus station. Paige had to hope that it would show her and Christopher something they could use. They kept following the security guard, heading through the bus depot to a series of back rooms and offices. One had a security station with a large screen in front of it, various views of the station mixed in with images that were obviously coming live from some of the buses.

"Here you go," the security guard said. "Do you think you can work it out from here? I'll need to go make sure all the press doesn't get in the way of the buses. My boss doesn't want the station to stop running on time."

"We're fine, thank you," Paige said. He'd given them more help than most people in this case.

Christopher was the one who sat down in front of the screen, quickly getting the hang of the controls for the different cameras, while establishing how to download the data for them to go through later. She saw him pick up a view for the entrance to the locker room, scrolling back until Peggy Cane came into view. She entered the locker room, and in just a few seconds, a man followed her in. He was wearing a long coat and a hat, both of which served to disguise his looks, making it hard to pick out much about him beyond the fact that he appeared to be a tall white male, maybe in his thirties.

That *had* to be the killer, although the cameras didn't catch the moment when he killed Peggy. He'd managed to find a blind spot in the locker room for that.

83

"Find another angle on him," Paige said.

"I'm trying," Christopher said. He pulled up another piece of footage, from a few seconds before, with Peggy Cane walking across the main concourse of the depot, and their suspect following close behind, his intent seeming obvious now that Paige knew it was him.

Again, though, his features didn't seem to be visible. He kept his head down and his hat obscured his features, making it impossible to get a clear view of him that might help to identify him.

They kept working their way back through the footage, the victim and her killer making their way across the depot in reverse, skipping from camera to camera. With each one, it was as if the suspect had a clear instinct for where those cameras were going to be, his face obscured by the hat all the time.

They followed the cameras all the way back to a bus. Paige stared at the screen, looking for just one frame of footage where the killer's face was clear, one instant that would let them know who he was, but she couldn't pick one out.

The bus number was clearly visible, and Paige saw Christopher go hunting for the footage from that bus. He found it, and now he scrolled back all the way to the point where Peggy first got on. The two of them started to watch that footage, searching for the moment when she had first run into her killer.

For a while, she was just sitting there in one of the front seats of the bus, taking up space with her arms spread wide to discourage anyone else from sitting there. Paige watched the bus fill up, little by little.

She saw the moment when the killer got aboard, and she hoped that now, there would be a shot of his face, but even here, he seemed to be able to obscure it; his instincts for the cameras' locations were so perfect that it seemed uncanny.

Paige saw him step in front of Peggy, making some kind of demand, perhaps for her seat. She saw him repeat his demand, and now the expression on the young woman's face was anything but friendly as she replied.

Paige saw the killer stalk down the bus in response, his movements stiff and angry even if she couldn't make out his features. Paige could see that was the moment when he'd decided to kill her, but she could barely believe it. It seemed so... small.

Was *that* what this had been about? An argument over a bus seat? Paige found herself thinking about Gisele Newbury's death too, and the erratic way she'd been driving according to Nick Lloyd. Was this somehow about such petty grievances?

Maybe, but Paige wasn't sure that it got her and Christopher any closer to answers.

"I think we've gotten what we're going to get from the footage," Christopher said. Paige could hear his frustration. "And we won't get the coroner's report until morning. Come on, it's getting late. We can do some work on the profile at the hotel, but we're not going to get anything more here tonight. We should call it a day for now and look at it fresh in the morning."

Paige knew he was right, but even so, the prospect worried her. Would this killer strike again in the night? Would he still be killing while they slept? Paige hoped not, but hoping was all she could do, because currently, they weren't any closer to catching him.

CHAPTER FIFTEEN

The hotel was a nondescript place on the fringes of Lexington that looked as though it pulled in a large horse racing clientele, judging by the photographs and prints of what Paige assumed were famous horses on the walls. Not being a fan of the sport herself, she didn't know.

The place was very comfortable looking, but also seemed as though it had deliberately gone out of its way to avoid any personality beyond the prints, as if suspecting that clients traveling for business didn't care about anything except clean, safe rooms that they could be gone from the moment morning came, and not wanting to spend any money on the place beyond that.

There was a small bar area, and to Paige's surprise, Christopher gestured to it as the two of them approached.

"Do you want to get a drink, Paige?"

It was uncharacteristic behavior from him; Christopher had been keeping his distance for a couple of cases now, apparently guessing the attraction that Paige felt and not wanting to provide any chance for anything to happen. Yet suddenly he wanted to have a drink with her? It was an offer that made Paige feel conflicted, a part of her wanting to keep up the careful distance that she'd maintained since she found out that Christopher had a wife, another part not wanting to make things awkward by turning down her partner.

She could have one drink, she supposed. It wouldn't make any difference, and in any case, it wasn't like anything was going to happen. Both she and Christopher were more careful than that. They were partners, and that was enough for both of them. It had to be.

"Sure," Paige said, heading over to the bar with him. The bartender was a good-looking young man in his twenties who flashed Paige a bright smile as she and Christopher approached, a note of obvious interest there that might have just been professional, or might have been something more. Paige found that she *wasn't* interested, though. She didn't react to every guy out there just because they were good looking. Only Christopher seemed to have that effect on her, and it had more to do with the way he was intelligent and kind, how he'd saved her life, and how he seemed to connect to her whatever the two of them were doing.

He *did* have that effect on her, though, making it hard to remember that they needed to keep distance between them.

"What will you have?" the bartender asked.

"Whiskey," Christopher said.

Paige shrugged. "Make that two."

Christopher raised an eyebrow. "I had you down as more of a white wine kind of woman."

"And what's one of those?" Paige asked, although truthfully, she'd only ordered the whiskey on a whim, to keep pace with her partner.

"Oh, you know, doesn't want to risk anything too strong in case it gets you slightly out of control," Christopher said. "I got the feeling that being in control of what's going on is important to you."

It was, most of the time. Mostly, Paige dreaded what might happen if she wasn't the person most in control of the situation. Now, though, Paige had the sudden urge to show Christopher that she wasn't that person. Or maybe she *wanted* to be a little bit out of control. Either way, she downed the whiskey in one smooth movement.

And then found herself coughing with the burn of it. A second burn, of embarrassment, flooded her face as she tried to get the coughing back under control, and Paige barely dared to look Christopher's way.

"Is the case getting to you?" Christopher asked her.

"What makes you say that?" Paige asked. He'd jumped right over the whiskey to the thing that actually *could* bother her.

"Partly because sitting there drinking whiskey isn't exactly characteristic, partly because I know you. I know how personally you take the investigations."

"What other way is there to take the deaths of three women?" Paige countered. "We're meant to be the ones catching the guy who did this. If we'd found a better lead…"

"We might still have ended up arresting the wrong guy," Christopher finished, with a serious expression. "Or it might have ended up taking longer to try to find the evidence we needed to make an arrest. We're doing more than anyone else is to try to catch the killer, Paige. And we *will* catch him. But it's more than that, isn't it?"

Paige nodded. She should have guessed that Christopher would end up seeing more than she wanted. He always seemed to.

"You were right before, I need to feel in control with these cases. After what happened to my father, feeling like I'm making progress on cases is the only way to feel as though I have any control over my life. And then there's my stepfather."

Her stepfather, who had never faced any legal retribution for the things that he'd done to Paige when she was a girl. Whose house her mother had gotten her out of the moment she found out.

"The bastard you punched?" Christopher said, and that memory brought a brief smile to Paige's face, which faded quickly under the weight of her memories. "What about him?"

"You heard him back then. He hinted that he knew something about my father's death."

"What could he possibly know?" Christopher asked. "Seriously, Paige. What could a guy like that know about a serial killer?"

"That's just it, I don't know," Paige said. "It's probably nothing. He probably didn't see anything or hear anything, but just with the fact that he's hinting at it, he continues to have power over me, and I hate that."

She shook her head, looking down into her glass. The whiskey was starting to hit her now. She'd hoped that it would take the edge off the anxiety she felt, but it didn't seem to be working that way for her.

"Enough about my messed-up life," Paige said, cupping the glass between her hands to roll it back and forth. "What about you? Tell me about the perfect life of Christopher Marriott."

Christopher downed his own drink. "Not so perfect."

"It seems pretty perfect from the outside."

"Meanwhile, from the inside, my marriage is falling apart." He set his glass down on the bar with a clink.

"What?" That took Paige completely by surprise. She'd met Jennifer when Christopher had brought her along to Paige's graduation from the FBI academy. She'd seemed like a wonderful person, and the two of them had seemed very happy together. "I thought you two were like the perfect couple."

It was one reason that Paige had been so careful around Christopher. She hadn't wanted to do anything that might jeopardize his perfect marriage. She hadn't wanted to be the woman who might do anything to break that up.

"Jennifer doesn't like that I'm away so much," Christopher said. "Or that I'm in danger running after criminals. She says I love my job more than I love her."

He sounded as though he couldn't work out if that was true or not. Paige doubted that it was. Christopher was committed to his work, certainly, but he also seemed like the kind of man who, once he was committed to someone, would put her ahead of anything else.

"But that's not true," Paige guessed.

"No, of course not," Christopher agreed. "But at the same time, I can't just give up being an FBI agent the way she wants. We're doing good work here, putting away killers who would otherwise go on to murder far more people. And Jennifer... I don't know, she's distant when I'm home, doesn't even seem like she cares most of the time. I'm half convinced she's cheating on me with someone when I'm not there. It's only when I'm away that she's calling me to tell me how much she loves me."

Paige thought that she could understand that part, at least. "Is it possible that she's pushing you away when you're close because she thinks you're going to go anyway? Then when you're further away, she feels how hard it is without you?"

"It's easy to forget that I have a psychologist for a partner," Christopher said with a wan smile. "I'm sorry, Paige, I shouldn't have said so much. You don't want to hear about my messed up personal life, or the way my wife is slowly drifting away from me."

Actually, there was nothing Paige wanted more than to hear everything about Christopher. She felt as though she could sit there and listen to every facet of his life, slowly looking deeper and deeper into the blue of his eyes while she did it...

And that was why she ought to go to bed now, before this went anywhere beyond a simple conversation between colleagues. Before the whiskey pushed them both to do something they shouldn't.

"We should go get some sleep," Paige said. "We have to start over in the morning and hope that we can find something new we can used to catch this killer."

Christopher looked over at her, and for a moment, Paige felt almost certain that he wanted to say more, wanted to persuade her to stay for another drink. He didn't, though. He seemed to sense, the same way that Paige did, that anything like that would be a bad idea right then.

"You're right," he said instead after a moment or two of consideration. "I'll see you in the morning, Paige."

He headed upstairs, and Paige could only watch him go with a strange mixture of relief and regret that nothing else had happened. Paige was quiet for several seconds, wondering if she should get another drink, but right then, that didn't feel like a good idea.

She suspected that if she went up to her room, she wouldn't be able to get to sleep straight away, so she got out her laptop to try to continue working instead, determined to try to use the time to make some progress. The only question was what she could work *on* that might help. Paige started by sending emails through to the FBI's techs, asking for them to get what they could of Peggy Cane's social media and other accounts for her to search through later. Paige didn't want to start trawling through the public parts of it all now, though, because the lack of connections between Meredith Park and Gisele Newbury already suggested that this wasn't about some link between the victims that she would be able to uncover online.

No, she needed to think of a new angle on this, something that wasn't obvious. She needed to talk about all of this and for Paige, there was one obvious person to call when it came to that.

Prof. Thornton picked up quickly when Paige called him.

"Hi Paige. How are you? I guess I should as *where* you are, too."

"Lexington," Paige said. Knowing Prof. Thornton, he would already know what she was looking at there. He liked to keep up with the news when it came to serial killers, because it fit in with his own work as a professor of criminal psychology.

"The stabbings with the small symbol left by them?" he said, proving her right. His research was broader than hers had been, but he still had an interest in serial killers and their work.

"That's right," Paige said, not surprised that her former Ph.D. supervisor knew about it. "We thought we'd caught the guy, but it turned out that he was elsewhere for one of the murders. Now, I'm trying to find a new angle on this. There has to be a way into it all, but I can't see what that might be."

Prof. Thornton didn't seem perturbed by the fact that Paige was coming to him for advice on an active investigation. Paige had done it before, after all, several times now.

"What have you tried so far?" he asked.

"Mostly, we've been following evidence from security footage," Paige said. "I thought I had a good idea about one of the victims maybe being targeted because of a road rage incident prior to her death, but that was the guy with the alibi."

"So, what's your profile on the killer?" Prof. Thornton asked.

"I... don't know," Paige admitted. "Probably male, probably young, but beyond that..."

Those were just standard assumptions to throw into any profile of a serial killer, based on the fact that the overwhelming majority of serial killers met those criteria. Paige knew that she needed far more than that, though.

"Paige, it sounds as though you've been going off chasing after the physical evidence to the exclusion of the thing you're actually *best* at," Prof. Thornton said, with the slightest note of rebuke in his voice. "You've spent extensive time researching serial killers in order to be able to understand them and their motives. You should be focusing on those. Do you know anything about the motives of this killer?"

"We saw him on security footage, arguing with Peggy Cane," Paige said. "And the guy we brought in said that Gisele Newbury was driving like a maniac, so maybe he wasn't the only person she upset. A killer who's over-reacting to minor annoyances?"

"And who would do that?" Prof. Thornton asked, in that patient tone that he'd always used in their tutorials, wanting her to work out the answers for herself rather than just handing them to her.

Paige wanted to just say a psychopath, but that wasn't quite right. Yes, psychopaths could be violent for little or no reason, but this kind of overreaction was more characteristic of someone with a very different set of traits.

"You're thinking Narcissistic Personality Disorder?" Paige said.

"I don't have enough information to make a professional judgement," Prof. Thornton pointed out, quick to get the caveat in. "Does it seem right to *you*, Paige?"

It did. Someone with NPD thought that they were essentially the center of the universe, or that everyone else was just a bit part player in the story of their life. Most thought that they were exceptional or special in some way: the cleverest, strongest, best human who had ever lived, or certainly better than any of the people they actually met. And when things went wrong for them, they always found someone else to blame.

Combine that narcissism with psychopathic tendencies, and they had a recipe for violence in response to the least insult. Maybe by this point, the killer was even seeking out conflict as an excuse to kill more victims. Maybe it reinforced his existing feelings of power?

It was speculation, but it seemed to fit better than any of the ways Paige had been thinking so far. The only question now was how Paige was going to use that starting point to get closer to the killer. She had an idea about that, though, one that would help her to understand his mindset better.

CHAPTER SIXTEEN

Paige woke the next morning more than ready to continue the investigation. She at least had an idea now of the kind of man they were looking for, and that energized her to continue the work of finding him, although she wasn't sure how much it narrowed things down. The world was full of narcissists. One look at social media demonstrated that. Finding a specific one whose narcissism was severe enough to constitute a reason to kill was something else entirely.

Paige needed to understand more about the killer, and what motivated him. Specifically, she wanted to understand the ways in which that motivation might change now that he'd killed. Paige thought that she understood the ways in which anger at Gisele Newbury might have driven him to kill in the first instance, but how had that turned into a killing spree that had so far claimed the lives of three victims?

Paige needed to understand that better, along with how a killer like that would select his victims. In previous cases, she'd been able to find imprisoned killers who had been able to provide her with insights, so maybe she could try something similar in this case. Maybe there would be someone near here she could question to try to get a better understanding of all of this.

Paige started to look for local secure psychiatric institutions, trying to find somewhere that would house killers. It didn't take long before she found the Brentview Hospital, there for the treatment and imprisonment of some of the most dangerous offenders Kentucky had to offer.

Paige started to compose an email to them, setting out who she was and what she wanted in the clearest terms she could think of. She was still trying to find ways to explain it all, when her phone rang. Paige didn't recognize the number, but answered anyway. She'd given her details to so many witnesses in this case that she didn't dare miss a call that might prove useful.

"Agent King?" a man's voice on the other end of the line said.

"Yes, who is this?" Paige kept her tone carefully neutral.

"My name is Giles Barnes, the blacksmith from the Renaissance Faire?"

Paige remembered. She'd asked him about the iron fleur-de-lis.

"Did you find something about the ornament?" she asked.

"Not that, but I think I've found out about the weapon you're looking for," Giles said. "Can you come over to the Ren-Faire? I'm here all day."

"I'll be right over," Paige promised, and ran to get Christopher. He would want to hear this, if they really did have a weapon profile.

*

The Renaissance Faire was a little quieter today than it had been the last time Paige had been there. It seemed that the initial excitement over the news of what had happened had passed, leaving behind a sense that people should stay away out of respect.

Paige doubted that it would last. Although her new job meant that she only saw locations in the immediate aftermath of deaths, she suspected that in the longer term normality washed back in, so that unless people already knew about a killing, eventually it wouldn't do anything to change their experience.

For now, though, the quietness was obvious, fewer people making their way between the stalls and the tents of the Renaissance Faire. The jesters and the knights were still there, playing their parts within the whole, but now, Paige could make out a couple of film crews moving among them, as if hoping that there would be more on the story that had gripped the news cycle over the last few days.

Paige saw a couple of those cameras turn her way as she walked, and she cursed, knowing that it was only a matter of time before there were reporters in front of her, wanting to know what she and Christopher were doing there at the Renaissance Faire again. Given their hostility so far, they might well start demanding why she and Christopher weren't making more progress.

"Don't worry," Christopher said as Paige tried to keep away from them. "We just tell them that we're following up on our earlier investigation here. There's no reason for them to think that there's anything new. We certainly don't have to tell them the real reason that we're here."

Paige knew he was right. Even so, she found herself keeping a careful eye on the camera crews as she made her way through the Renaissance Faire. She decided to make her path deliberately circuitous, looking around for any of the people she and Christopher

94

had spoken to the last time they were here. She didn't want to give away whatever information they got about the murder weapon too easily. It felt like the kind of thing that, if it got out, might risk spawning copycats, or force the killer to change his methods. Paige didn't want to risk either.

She stopped at a jester, who looked slightly worried, as if suspecting that Paige was about to chase him down and arrest him, the way she and Christopher had with Steve the knight.

"Sorry," she said. "We don't want to disturb you. We were just wondering if you've remembered anything else about the day Meredith was killed since we were last here. Any detail, no matter how small, might be useful."

"No, I'm sorry," he said. At least he wasn't trying his medieval jester routine on them this time. "I've been asking myself about it constantly, wondering if there was anything I could have done, but... no, there's nothing."

"That's all right," Paige said. "We just have to check."

She wanted to make it sound like everything she was doing there was just routine, so that the press wouldn't have a reason to crowd around too closely. Paige made her way to the next person they had spoken to on their first visit to the Renaissance Faire, the archery instructor, trying to circle closer and closer to the blacksmith, little by little.

They made it to his tent, the heat of his forge intense there. He was concentrating on the billet of steel he was currently holding using tongs, hammering it into shape with sharp, intense blows that rang from the metal.

Paige walked into his eyeline, not knowing if he would hear her over the sound of the hammering if she just called out to him. The blacksmith stopped his work as he saw her, setting aside what he was working on.

"Agent King, you came."

"You remember Agent Marriott?" Paige said.

"Of course. Thank you both for coming down like this. Only with something like this, it's easier to show you than to just say it."

"Say what?" Christopher asked.

Paige did her best to explain. "Because Giles here knows about medieval weapons, I asked him if he'd ever seen anything that might cause the wounds that the coroner has been finding on the victims."

Christopher didn't look entirely happy. "I thought that was information we might hold back."

"If we did that, we wouldn't have a chance to actually find the murder weapon," Paige said. She looked over to the blacksmith. "You *did* find the murder weapon?"

The blacksmith nodded, and Paige thought she could see Christopher's slight disapproval melting away in the face of that. He wanted new information on this case as badly as Paige did. Paige could feel the excitement building in her at the thought of finally knowing what weapon they should look for when it came to this case. Once they knew that, there was at least a faint possibility that they would be able to use the information to link it back to the killer.

"At least, I think so. Over here," the blacksmith said, leading the way to a bench. A dagger sat there, or at least the blade and cross guard of one. It didn't look finished to Paige. "I made this last night, to designs I found in a couple of old books on medieval weaponry. It doesn't currently have a handle, and this is just a dummy model that we'll use for the knight fights, so there's no edge, but it should be able to give you an idea of what it looks like."

Paige could hear the note of nervousness in the blacksmith's voice, and she suspected that part of the reason he hadn't finished the weapon was because he'd realized that having an exact copy of the murder weapon lying around would look a little suspicious. At the very least, it would lead to Paige and Christopher asking how long he'd had it, just in case he was trying to pass off the actual murder weapon as a mere copy of it.

Paige tested the point. It was indeed blunt. This hadn't been used to kill anyone, but it had seemed safest to check, just to eliminate the possibility. She looked over the blade. It was slender but square sided.

"So this was a thrusting weapon only?" Paige asked.

The blacksmith nodded. "It's called a misericord. It's similar to a stiletto or a rondel dagger, but it wouldn't have had sharpened edges the way they might. We have records of them dating back all the way to the 12th century."

"So the idea was... what?" Christopher said, looking the weapon over with a professional eye. "To punch through the gaps in armor?"

Paige saw the blacksmith nod. She was impressed that Christopher could take one look at a weapon and instantly understand what its best tactical use was.

"Usually through the visor," the blacksmith said.

"Not through the heart?" Paige asked, because that was what had happened with the three victims so far.

"A knight's armor wouldn't have made that a good target," the blacksmith explained. "A breastplate would probably stop this dead, and even a coat of mail backed up by padding would slow it down."

That was an interesting discrepancy. Did the killer not know that part, or did he just not care that much for historical accuracy, in spite of the symbols he left behind?

"The misericord had another use, though," the blacksmith said. "Its name comes from the old French for mercy. It was used to kill badly wounded knights who had suffered injuries in battle. In judicial duels, it might be used to deliver the last blow to someone who had lost."

"Judicial duels?" Christopher said.

"Trial by combat," the blacksmith clarified. "In most places, the private duel between individuals was banned quite early in the Middle Ages; it was never legal in England, for example, but there would be various forms of trial by combat, sometimes with different weapons depending on the accusation."

Paige found herself wondering how relevant that was. Was the killer someone who would know the history of the weapon as well as the blacksmith did? What did the inclusion of the fleur-de-lis mean? Did it mean anything, or was the killer just collecting a set of symbols that only made sense within the confines of his twisted mind?

No, Paige wasn't going to believe that there was nothing to be gained here. This was meaningful to the killer, which meant that understanding that meaning would help to bring them closer to him.

"Thank you," she said to the blacksmith. She took pictures of the misericord he'd made from as many angles as possible. "You've been very helpful."

She moved away from the blacksmith's tent with Christopher, so that she could talk to him openly about the details of the case without being overheard.

"So we know what the murder weapon is," he said.

"I think we might know more than that," Paige replied. "This is a killer using an ancient symbol of royalty, striking people down with a weapon that might be used after a duel, and reacting to the least insult with deadly force. This is someone who thinks they're special, they're royalty, they can mete out what they see as justice to anyone who insults them."

Christopher was silent for several seconds as he considered it. Paige guessed that it was a lot to take on board all at once.

"Ok," Christopher said. "I can see that."

"I think we're dealing with a narcissist," Paige said.

"Not a psychopath?"

"It's possible to be both, but people with Narcissistic Personality Disorder focus more on their own importance, to the exclusion of everyone else."

"Can we use that to locate the killer?" Christopher asked.

"Maybe, but I want to get into his head more. There's a local secure mental institution that has several patients with NPD. I think if I talk to one of them, I might be able to work out more about what's going on with this killer's pathology."

"Are you sure that's a good idea?" Christopher asked. "The last couple of times you've done this, you've been attacked."

"But I also got insights that helped with the case," Paige pointed out.

"I… can't argue with that," Christopher admitted.

"I need to do this," Paige said. "If someone else is killed, and I don't try everything I can to help, then I'll feel like it's on me."

She saw Christopher give in.

"All right, but I'm coming too."

CHAPTER SEVENTEEN

The Brentview Hospital was a large and imposing building that looked to Paige as if it had been built sometime in the 19th century, then adapted as required to meet the needs of the inmates it housed. It had a kind of faded grandeur to it that made it look more like a university library than a psychiatric institution, its red brick walls tangled with ivy, its grounds set out with neat lawns and gardens. Paige could see some of the inmates there working in the gardens, possibly as part of some kind of therapy.

The interior of the building was painted in pastel colors that should have been soothing but mostly just seemed institutional to Paige after her time working in a place similar to this. It was a reminder of the times she'd spent in the St. Just Institute, having to sit down opposite some of the worst criminals to assess them, trying to get them to talk about themselves.

She was going to have to do it again today, if she was going to get more information that might let them truly understand the man she and Christopher were trying to catch.

Of course, there were limits to how much she might get. Hopefully, she would understand more about his motives and methods, but it wasn't as if all serial killers knew one another. Interviewing killers here wouldn't necessarily lead Paige straight to his door, but she hoped that it would give her some insights.

A doctor met them at the door, ID clipped to his pocket, sleeves rolled up above the elbow. He was a little shorter than Christopher, with wavy dark hair and glasses.

"I'm Dr. Spiel," he said. "Are you Agent King?"

Paige showed her ID. In a place like this, security mattered even if it appeared to be a more relaxed environment than a normal prison.

"That's right," Paige said. "And this is my partner, Agent Marriott."

Her partner. Paige and Christopher had been through so much together by now that it was actually beginning to feel real when Paige said it. They'd saved one another's lives, taken down several deadly killers, and worked together in almost perfect harmony. Only the lingering problem of the attraction Paige felt towards Christopher was there to cause trouble between them, creating distance even as they worked smoothly together.

"It's good to meet you both," Dr. Spiel said. He led the way through into a reception area that was as bright and clean as that of any private health spa, so that Paige might have mistaken it for one if it weren't for the security doors leading off from it, each obviously leading to a different wing of the hospital.

"In your email, you said that you wanted to talk to patients we had whose Narcissistic Personality Disorder had resulted in violence?" Dr. Spiel raised an eyebrow. "I must say, that is a highly unusual request, Agent King. The patients in our care are here because they pose a danger to the public or to themselves. In general, we don't allow people who aren't trained medical professionals to just come in to speak to them."

"If it helps, I *am* a medical professional," Paige said. "I completed a Ph.D. on the motivations of serial killers while working at an institution very similar to this one. We're not here to disturb your patients, Dr. Spiel, but we *do* think that talking to one of them might help us to understand the motivations of a killer who has so far claimed three lives."

For a moment, Paige thought that Dr. Spiel might still say no, but then he nodded.

"Very well, we'll go through to my office, and I'll have a patient brought to us. I will remain throughout, to ensure the safety of you both and the patient."

He led the way to one of the security doors, punching in a code to get through. There was a burly orderly on the other side, acting as a guard.

"Micah, could you bring Nadia to my office, please? The FBI wishes to speak with her."

He led the way through the facility. It did its best to seem like a calming, healing environment, but it was hard to avoid the locked security doors and the cameras staring down, the presence of orderlies there to restrain dangerous prisoners or the constant sense of violence that hung in the air. Paige could hear a couple of shouts of anger, and the sound of someone sobbing, as she followed the doctor through the secure institution, to his office.

That office might have been the office of an academic professor except that there was nothing sharp, or potentially dangerous, in open view. There were bookshelves with rows of neat volumes on different aspects of psychology, a computer set up on a desk, and a small circle of comfortable chairs that wouldn't have looked out of place with someone giving a tutorial to a group of students. Except that it presumably wasn't students who sat there, but the inmates, there for psychological assessments or therapy sessions.

"You say you completed a PhD in criminal psychology?" Dr. Spiel said, as he gestured for Paige and Christopher to take a seat. "What on?"

"A case study on Adam Riker," Paige said.

She saw the doctor's eyes widen slightly. He'd obviously read about Adam, the killer who tied his victims and left them to slowly suffocate.

"That was you? I heard about him escaping, but…"

"But we caught him again," Christopher said, cutting in, as if he were worried about the effect that revisiting everything with Adam would have on Paige.

Paige was grateful for it. She still had nightmares about following Adam into the woods, and about the moment where he'd tied up her mother and tried to get Paige to kill her. She still found herself thinking about the moment when she'd shot him, and he'd tried to make her finish him off, telling Paige that she was just the same as him inside.

Paige had to struggle to push back thoughts of Adam. She told herself that she was there to do a job, and that she would need to pay attention, because she was about to be around another dangerous criminal, who might make her pay for any slip.

Paige took a seat on one of the comfortable chairs, waiting.

"What can you tell me about the prisoner you're having brought here?" she asked.

"Patient, not prisoner. We are attempting to treat the residents here." The doctor's tone turned it into a rebuke.

"And will this *patient* ever be getting out?" Christopher asked.

"Possibly, if we find a way to change her condition," Dr. Spiel said. "But realistically… no."

"Nadia has NPD?" Paige asked.

The doctor nodded. "Manifesting in violent behavior when she doesn't get her way. She believes herself to be the only truly important person in the world. Everyone else is there to do things for her. Occasionally, she seems to lapse into solipsism, with the idea that she is the only truly real person, although those bouts tend not to last."

101

"Because if other people aren't real, their attention isn't worth anything?" Paige guessed.

"Exactly."

"Why is she here?" Paige asked.

"Nadia killed two people," Dr. Spiel said. "They had upset her in ways that really only made sense to Nadia. She executed the crimes quite brilliantly, not leaving any physical evidence."

"So how was she caught?" Paige asked.

"She boasted about it. She told people about it to make her feel superior, and to try to make them afraid of her. One the police knew to look her way, they were able to match the murder weapon to a gun she possessed. At that point, she didn't so much confess as rush to tell the police every detail."

As the doctor said that, a knock came at the door.

"Come in," Dr. Spiel said.

The door opened, revealing an orderly and a woman in her thirties, dark haired, with large brown eyes and features that gave her a mischievous look even while she was just standing there. She was wearing gray sweatpants and a hooded top, a disposable, institutional uniform that was probably standard issue. Her hands were cuffed in front of her. She looked around the way an actor might when first walking on stage to applause. It was as if, the moment she saw Paige, Christopher, and Dr. Spiel, they became her audience.

"Dr. Spiel!" she said, as if they were old friends, and not doctor and patient. She rushed forward, grabbing his hand and shaking it with both of hers, slightly too long.

Paige recognized it as a simple piece of boundary testing or assertion of dominance, a way of Nadia saying that she could do what she wanted, and there was nothing the doctor could do to stop her.

"Nadia, we've spoken about this," Dr. Spiel said, pulling back. Nadia seemed to enjoy the effort it took him. She obviously liked embarrassing people.

"Did we? I don't remember. And I feel I would remember if we did. I have an exceptional memory."

Paige could see the note of exasperation on Dr. Spiel's face.

"Yes, Nadia, we did."

"No we didn't."

She sat down on one of the chairs without waiting to be asked, crossing her legs, and giving Paige a look so direct that it was uncomfortable. With a lot of psychopaths, Paige wouldn't have looked away, but with Nadia, she made a point of doing so, letting her have the small victory that someone with NPD would probably need.

"Who are they?" Nadia asked. She acted as if she were in charge of the whole situation. "I didn't ask to see anyone."

"They're with the FBI," Dr. Spiel said.

Nadia instantly looked bored. "Why would I want to speak with the FBI?"

Paige tried to come up with something quickly. If this patient decided that she didn't want to talk to her or Christopher, then the two of them would have come out here for nothing. Maybe they would be able to talk to a different patient, but Paige doubted it, when Dr. Spiel had already warned them against disturbing his patients.

"We think that your insight could really be invaluable," Paige said. "Without your help, we might never be able to solve this."

She wasn't appealing to any sense of altruism from this patient because she doubted that there was anything there to appeal to. But she could make Nadia feel like helping made her the most important person in the room.

"What can't you solve?" Nadia asked, looking vaguely interested.

"There's a man killing people. People who have insulted him."

"Why should I care about this man?" Nadia asked. "What's in it for me if I help?"

Paige found herself trying to think of something that might catch the killer's attention long enough to get her to help. She wasn't in a position to offer Nadia her freedom, or even better conditions. There was one thing she realized that she could offer, though.

"I'll make sure that the press hears that you were involved," Paige said. "I'll make sure that everyone knows we only caught this guy because of you."

That seemed to catch her attention.

"What do you want to know?"

"What was it like for you, when you killed? What made you want to do it?"

Nadia shrugged. "It was easy. Why wouldn't it be easy? They weren't anybody important. The *stupid* thing is that they put me in here for it. It wasn't like I did anything wrong."

Did she actually believe that? Possibly, if she truly thought that she was the only person who mattered.

"Do you know how they treat me here?" Nadia said. "They make me talk to idiots, and they ignore me all the time. They act like I'm *ordinary*."

It was one thing knowing that this was the way a narcissist thought, but it was quite another to see it in person.

"Why did you tell people about what you'd done?" Paige asked. That was a part that had caught her attention about Nadia's crimes.

The killer shrugged, though, not answering.

"You wanted people to know, didn't you?" Paige said. "You needed them to know, so it didn't matter that you were confessing to a crime."

"It wasn't really a crime," Nadia said. "I explained all this to my lawyer, but he didn't get it right in front of the court. The police told lies about me."

"Can we focus on the man we're trying to catch?" Christopher said.

It was a mistake. Nadia glared at him.

"This is boring now. I don't want to talk to you anymore. Take me back out of here."

She said it as if she were in complete command, but Paige suspected that there was no way now that she was going to change her mind.

"Nadia," she said.

"No, we're done here." Nadia stood up and headed for the door. The orderly who had brought her there moved to intercept her, and Dr. Spiel looked over to Paige as if wondering what he should do.

"Let her go," Paige said. "It's obvious that Nadia doesn't know anything that might help."

"I do," Nadia snapped back. "Of course I do. I know plenty of things that might help. Like... how is this guy letting people know what he's done? How is he making sure people know it's him? You see, I know more than all of you."

Paige signaled to the orderly to let her go from the room.

"Well, that was a waste of time," Dr. Spiel said, as Nadia left. "And now I'll have to deal with an agitated patient, for nothing."

"On the contrary," Paige said. "I think that we've learned something very useful indeed."

CHAPTER EIGHTEEN

Back at the FBI field office, Paige did her best to explain her idea to Christopher, sitting across from him in a small side office, trying to show how it might work.

"I think there's a chance that the killer might try to find a way to boast about what he's doing," she said.

"Based on a conversation with a completely different killer? Can you generalize from one to another like that?"

Paige could hear the skepticism there, but she wasn't about to let it stop her.

"If this were some academic study, no," Paige said, "but here? I think Nadia was a useful source of inspiration, at least."

"Are you going to tell her that?" Christopher asked, cocking his head to one side. "It seems like she wants the attention."

"That's my point," Paige replied. "Some serial killers send notes, or try to taunt the police. I think this one needs more attention than that."

"So you don't think the fleur-de-lis ornaments will be enough for them?" Christopher called up a photograph of one of them. "I feel like we should be looking deeper into that side of things. Maybe if we can find out where they were made, that might lead us to him. Someone buying a bunch of iron fleur-de-lis ornaments can't be that common."

"But it's also not the kind of thing someone would keep records of," Paige pointed out. "Unless he's having them custom made."

"Maybe he is." Christopher shrugged. "Either way, it's our best piece of physical evidence. I want to at least check."

Paige was surprised that Christopher wasn't just going along with her idea. Previously in their partnership, it had seemed that he'd been ready to follow along with most of her ideas. Why was *this* one a step too far?

"I still think though that the ornaments won't be enough for him," Paige said. "We went to see Nadia to get a real feel for what a killer with NPD might be like. Do you really think someone like that would settle for a cryptic calling card?"

"Maybe, if they thought that it proved they were cleverer than anyone else, able to leave clues and still not get caught."

"Even there," Paige insisted. "I'd expect them to start to escalate. The would want to prove that they could go even further."

Christopher stopped and stared at her, with a serious expression. "Paige, do you really think that the killer has just... what? Written a confession somewhere for the world to see?"

Paige shook her head. "Maybe not anything as obvious as that, but there will be *something*. A killer like this thrives on the attention. More than that, I think they'll want to *engage* with the attention. They'll want to be in the middle of everything, basking in the notoriety. I just have to work out how they'll do that."

Christopher still didn't look entirely convinced. "That seems... kind of nebulous. I'm not saying don't pursue it, but while you're doing that, I need to check out the fleur-de-lis angle. If Sauer hears that we ignored it and someone else dies, he'll want to know why."

That stopped Paige, her surprise overtaking her. She'd thought that Christopher was handling the pressure of this case, but that last comment definitely suggested that it was starting to get to him.

"Is everything ok?" Paige asked him.

Christopher looked as though he might just say that everything was fine, but he could obviously see the way that Paige was watching his features, able to read the tension there.

He shook his head. "It's just everything with the local PD. By standing off like this, they're putting pressure on us to solve the case quicker, saying that they could do things better. I've already had a dozen emails from reporters requesting interviews about why we're not making progress in the case."

Paige hadn't known that. She guessed that Christopher was doing his best to shield her from that side of things.

"So you want to put our efforts into the fleur-de-lis?" Paige said. She didn't actually want to give up on the angle she thought she'd found, but she also didn't want to put Christopher in a position where he had pressure from every side because of her.

"No, it's ok," Christopher said. "We'll work quicker if we split up on this. I'll try to look deeper into the fleur-de-lis, you follow up on your idea that the killer might come out into the open for the attention."

He still didn't sound as though he believed that it would work, but at least he was giving Paige the space she needed to look into it.

Of course, it meant that there was a new pressure on Paige to find results. She'd been the one to insist that they go over to the psychiatric institution to talk to one of the patients. She'd been the one to suggest this new line of inquiry. Now, she was the one who was going to spend time looking at it rather than helping Christopher with what seemed like a more solid, tangible aspect of the case.

Every minute that Paige spent on this was potentially time in which the killer might strike again. She didn't know if he was killing on a schedule, or simply reacting to the small insults that came his way in the course of everyday life. If it was the latter, then Paige had no way of knowing whether the killer would target someone in the next ten minutes, or leave it another day before he struck. Paige doubted that it would be longer than that, though. Spree killers accelerated, they didn't fade away.

That raised the worry that if Paige was wasting time on this hunch, it might cost another woman her life.

Why was this killer only targeting women? He didn't seem to have a preferred victim type in terms of age or looks, so why wasn't he targeting men as well? The answer to that seemed obvious to Paige: his method relied on being able to physically overpower someone quickly. He might believe that he was special and important, but some part of him had decided that he couldn't risk taking on larger, stronger men. He was deliberately sticking to targets he believed to be weaker than himself. There might be other reasons too, of course: a strong streak of misogyny, perhaps, or just a pathology that was only about punishing women for the mistake of insulting him. Maybe that was even linked to his apparent fascination with the medieval.

Paige didn't know, but she was determined to find any trace of him, wherever he was.

The question now was how she would go about finding someone like that. Paige guessed that in the modern world, someone wanting to announce what they were doing would do it somewhere on the internet, but where?

Paige started by searching for the case. That was faintly depressing, because the first hits to come up were all news stories with headlines like.

FBI stumped as killer claims third victim!
and
Lexington PD pushed out by FBI as local women die

It seemed that the local police force's approach of standing back and waiting for Paige and Christopher to fail was starting to bear fruit. She hated that they were playing games with the lives of innocent people like this. If they'd helped, maybe that would have been enough to catch the killer by now.

Paige forced herself to click on those stories, ignoring the main body of the text and skipping through to the comment sections. She had to brace herself for that part, because she thought she had a pretty good idea of just how negative it was going to be about her and Christopher in there.

Paige quickly found that she didn't know the half of it.

Have you seen that woman agent who has been showing up at the scenes? Hope the killer targets her next. Maybe then the FBI will send some real agents to solve this.

All of this is just faked, there to let the FBI come in and take over from local police.

The level of bile in the comments that followed was enough to make Paige feel a wave of disgust. It made it hard to wade through them all, trying to ignore the chatbots and the trolls to look for anyone who was expressing admiration for the killer, or even claiming outright to be them.

There were a depressing number of fans of the killer out there already. Paige guessed that most of them were doing it just to provoke a response, but she still had to follow up on each account, trying to work out if it might have any connection to the killer. That meant trying to track other comments made by the user elsewhere, looking for others that might praise the killer, or hint at knowledge that the general public didn't have.

It was thankless work, and Paige found herself wondering if maybe Christopher had a point. Maybe they did need to focus on the things that were more tangible, and follow up on the physical evidence.

Then she came across a comment by a poster calling himself "Fleur-de-lis 1234", which said:

This killer is clearly a superior human being. He ignores the petty morality of the world and imposes his own, with the most beautiful deaths. More on my web page.

There was a web address linked to the comment and Paige guessed that it was about a fifty-fifty shot that it was some kind of virus, but she had to know for sure if this was their guy. She clicked on it and instantly found herself on a dark, brooding webpage, decorated with a fleur-de-lis design that was far too familiar.

Paige read through the webpage, barely able to believe that it was there. She found a selection of Gothic looking photographs of castles, torture implements, and women in heavy dark makeup. Her real interest, though, was caught by a section that called itself a serial novel. It was titled "How I could have killed them better."

Paige clicked on it and started to read.

As I approached Meredith, she turned to me, begging for her life. Such weakness. Such stupidity. Couldn't she see that I'd already made my decision? I closed in on her with the knife in my hand, feeling the tautness of my skin around my knuckles as I gripped it tightly...

Paige could only sit there and stare at it, barely able to believe what she was seeing. She skipped to another section.

Gisele was an affront to me from the moment that I saw her. She had to die. She behaved as if she mattered, as if she were the most important person in the world. I couldn't allow that. I had to show her that the world runs the way I allow it to, no one else...

"Christopher," Paige said. "I think you need to see this."

Christopher came over. "What is it? What have you found?"

"There's a guy here with a website where he writes about the murders," Paige said. "He's writing as if he's the killer, and he's made a bunch of comments praising him online, making it sound as if he has this world changing agenda."

Christopher looked over her shoulder at the writing there, starting to read.

"And the guy calls himself fleur-de-lis 1234 online," Paige said.

"It's definitely suspicious," Christopher said. He clicked through onto the site, and now Paige saw that there was a small link entitled "About the Author".

No, he couldn't really have been stupid enough to do that, could he?

Paige clicked on it, and a page came up, showing a name and a photograph, along with what seemed to be a pretty standard author blurb.

Fleur-de-lis is a pen name of Julius Bryant, an author for more than ten years. His works have been on bestseller lists around the world and have won many prestigious awards. For agent inquiries please use the contact form below.

Paige was more interested in the photograph, of a lean, thin faced man with dark hair. There was something familiar about that man, something that made Paige certain that she'd seen him before.

It took several seconds for her to work out where, but when she did, Paige quickly started clicking through her laptop's files, calling up security footage, looking for the section she wanted.

She found the image she was looking for in the footage taken from the restaurant the day Meredith Park had died. She paused it, turning the screen to Christopher.

"There, you see that guy? He was there in the restaurant before Meredith left, and he was staring at her strangely. I'm not imagining it, am I?"

Christopher shook his head. "You're not imagining it, Paige."

There, in the footage from the restaurant, was the same man whose features currently sat in a head shot on the author bio section of his website. Julius Bryant had been there in the restaurant with Meredith. He'd written about killing her.

They had to find him, right away.

"I'm looking up Julius Bryant," Christopher said. "It looks like he's an author who was dropped by his publisher a while back for poor sales and plagiarism. There's no address here with the DMV, but I *can* see a thing where he's talking at a convention for online authors. It's in Lexington."

"We need to get over there," Paige said. "Before he has a chance to kill anyone else."

CHAPTER NINETEEN

The convention was at a small hotel on the outskirts of Lexington which looked to Paige as though it had seen better days. It was the kind of place that businesspeople might book for an overnight stay if they were moving on in the morning, but that no one would really stay at if they were planning to see more of the city, or if they were there on vacation.

She guessed that conventions were part of the lifeblood of a place like that, including some pretty important ones. Certainly, looking at the details of the convention online, the organizers seemed to be making a big deal of it.

Paige read aloud as Christopher drove.

"This is Kentucky's biggest and best convention for online creators of all kinds, featuring self-publishing, online only authors, musicians and creatives from fields as disparate as e-sports and crafting."

"That sounds like we're going to be walking into the middle of a lot of people there," Christopher said.

Paige nodded. "It also sounds a bit… unfocused. Like they're trying to get everyone they can from *wherever* they can."

Put like that, maybe it wasn't such a big thing after all. Maybe they were having to cast their net wide because they couldn't get the numbers to justify a convention otherwise.

When they reached the hotel, it was clear that this wasn't something on the scale of say a major comic convention, but the parking lot was still pretty full, and there were still plenty of people hanging around outside, talking to one another in the open air.

Paige ignored them; they weren't the suspect she and Christopher were here to find. If Julius Bryant was scheduled to speak at this convention, then he would be somewhere inside.

They entered the hotel, and were immediately met by a greeter standing at a folding table full of name badges. The greeter was a young woman with purple hair wearing jeans and a yellow t-shirt with the words "Content Creator" emblazoned across the front.

"Hi!" she said in a slightly too cheerful tone. "If you're here for the convention, this is the place to pick up your name badges. What kind of content do you create?"

Paige flashed her badge. "We're not here for the convention. We're looking for someone who is speaking here. Julius Bryant?"

"Oh, him," the young woman said, with a slight note of distaste. "He's speaking on a panel at the moment, all about finding new ways to make a killing in crime fiction online. I'm pretty sure the pun was his idea."

She made it sound as if she expected the FBI to be there to arrest him for that, if for nothing else.

"And where can we find that panel?" Paige asked.

In reply, the greeter handed her a folded map of the hotel, apparently designed to make the whole place seem far larger than it actually was. The details of the different panels and events in each room were set out in small sidebars.

"It should all be on here," she said. "I think the details of who's speaking on what panel are on the back."

It was obvious that she hadn't bothered to memorize who was where, or at least, she hadn't paid much attention to exactly where Julius Bryant was.

A part of Paige wanted to rush off in pursuit of their suspect, but she took the time to ask a couple more questions.

"Did you meet Julius Bryant when he signed in here?" Paige asked.

The greeter shrugged. "I guess."

"What did you make of him?" Paige asked.

The greeter looked a little uncomfortable, as if she didn't want to risk saying anything unpleasant about one of the speakers there.

"You're not going to get into any trouble," Paige promised her. "We just want to hear the truth."

"Honestly? He kind of creeps me out," the greeter said. "He walked in acting like he was the most important guy in the world, and I was kind of in a rush, so I just pushed his name badge his way without really stopping to talk, and he looked at me like... well, like I'd committed some unforgivable sin, or something."

Paige looked over at Christopher. To her, that sounded like exactly the kind of thing the killer would have done. Was it possible that Julius Bryant had just decided on his next victim? Was he only waiting for an opportunity to get this young woman alone before he struck?

Paige didn't know for sure, but it was one more reason for her and Christopher to talk to Julius as soon as possible.

They started to make their way through the conference, past crowds of people who were talking about online fiction, and other forms of content creation. The hotel's conference rooms had signs outside, setting out what was running in them and when. Paige walked past one where the current topic was "Generating ideas through combination and atomization," stepped past another in which a panel seemed to be discussing the similarities between e-sports streaming and chess content creation, and soon found herself standing outside a room where the sign said that it was playing host to a panel on "Making a Killing in Online Crime Fiction."

"This is the one," Christopher said, reaching for the handle.

"How do we play this?" Paige asked. "Do we go in and wait until we can get him alone before we approach him?"

Christopher shook his head, though. "There's too much chance of him spotting us and taking an opportunity to slip away. If this is our killer, there's a real danger that he'll take the opportunity to strike again. No, we're going to go in there and ask to speak to him directly, then react from there. If he comes quietly, fine. If he runs, we take him down and arrest him. We can't take the risk of him getting away."

Paige could only agree with that. Having read Julius's online story, it seemed obvious that he was already thinking about ways to commit murder in more perfect ways. Was that a part of it? Was he not quite satisfied with his kills each time? Did he always have to seek out the next victim, trying to live up to some ideal that only existed in his imagination?

Paige couldn't give him a chance to do that.

She and Christopher strode into the conference hall. There were rows of chairs set out there, although the sheer number of them was a little optimistic. There were probably only about a dozen people listening to the panel.

A stage sat at the front with a table for the trio of panelists there. Paige recognized Julius Bryant at the center of the panel, flanked by a man and a woman who both had physical copies of their books set in front of them, as if wanting to take any opportunity to advertise. Julius had a laptop open in front of him. Julius was a lean, dark haired man with a long face and striking features. He was currently wearing a suit, and had a long coat slung over the back of his chair. Was that the coat that the killer had been wearing in the video footage from the bus?

The two authors next to Julius looked faintly bored as Julius was speaking, as if he'd been going on for some time now, and they were just waiting for a chance to speak themselves.

"What I'm saying is that to do anything truly original in such a saturated field, we must be prepared to embrace reality. We must be prepared to do the unthinkable, to step across lines that previously seemed inviolable. The only way to get attention, when so many eyes are elsewhere, is to do the things that people *cannot* look away from."

Paige couldn't help herself. She stepped forward, with her badge held out. "Is that why you've killed three people, Julius?"

"Questions are reserved for the *end* of the panel," Julius shot back. It was utterly incongruous, as if he simply didn't acknowledge that Paige had any authority.

Paige glanced around and saw several phones pointed her way, obviously recording. Of course they would be, in the middle of a conference dedicated to content creators.

Still, Paige was determined to try again. "Julius Bryant, I'm Agent King, with the FBI. My colleague is Agent Marriott. We need to speak to you, right now."

He gave her an annoyed look. "As you can see, I am right in the middle of a panel. If you wish to speak to me, I can come find you afterwards, assuming that I have any time to do it."

Paige looked over to Christopher, who shook his head pretty much as she'd guessed that he would. They'd already discussed this, and Julius's deluded sense of self-importance only made it more likely that he was their guy. They couldn't let him have a chance to get out of there.

"I'm going to have to insist," Paige said, moving forward.

A couple of the small group of fans stood up, moving into her path.

"Hey, you can't do this," one of them said. He was a big, bearded man wearing a plaid shirt. "You can't just mess with Julius. Don't you know he's one of the most brilliant writers of this generation?"

"*The* most brilliant!" Julius said, clearly unable to help himself as his self-regard took over.

"Step out of the way, or I'll arrest you for obstruction," Paige said.

The big man snorted. "I'd like to see you try."

He reached out towards Paige, and the moment his hand touched her, she grabbed it and twisted painfully, using the lock to force him to one side. She pushed him away and continued to head for the stage. Another of Julius's fans got in the way, though.

"This is just trying to shut down free speech! Artists should be free to make art!"

"Not if they're killing people to do it," Paige said, but the man still didn't move.

Christopher was there then, forcing the man aside with his greater size and weight. It created a gap for the two of them to try to get to the stage.

Meanwhile, Julius seemed to be typing furiously on his laptop.

"The FBI agents approached the stage, as I had known they would, every move they made predicted, every moment of this predetermined through my own genius..."

"He's *writing* this?" Christopher said.

Paige shrugged. "I guess after writing the details of three murders, writing his arrest for them only makes sense."

Paige still didn't want to allow him to do it, though. She hopped up onto the stage, but Julius leapt up too, holding his laptop as he backed away.

"Dictation mode on," he said, and then kept narrating. "The FBI agents had reached the stage now, their pinched features focused on me in expressions of hate, determined to stop me at any cost. I backed away, knowing that I would find a way to escape their clutches, no matter what they tried. I saw my chance, and leapt."

He hopped down off the stage, wading into the chairs set out in the hall as if they were a sea. Paige set off after him, moving quicker, hurdling the chairs as she tried to close the distance.

"No, this is impossible, you can't catch me!" Julius cried out, even as Paige got close enough to throw herself at him in a tackle that was far less elegant than she might have wanted.

The two of them went crashing down among the chairs, sending them scattering. Julius started to fight back, still narrating the whole thing as he went for the benefit of his computer.

"I struck out! I kicked at her, and..."

And the very fact that he'd just said he was going to do it gave Paige plenty of time in which to dodge. She slipped aside from the strike, and then wrenched Julius onto his stomach. It was a fight to get his arms behind his back, but Christopher was there then, helping. Between them, they managed to get cuffs onto the writer.

Paige gasped out the words as she tried to get her breath back. "Julius Bryant, you're under arrest."

CHAPTER TWENTY

They took Julius Bryant back to the field office of the FBI, and Paige wasn't entirely surprised to find the press there waiting for them.

"Have you made an arrest, agents?" one of the reporters called out. "Is *this* one going to be the real killer?"

There was a pointed note to the question, obviously trying to insinuate that they hadn't managed to do their jobs before.

"Reports say that you dragged this man out of a conference where he was giving a talk," another said. "Were you trying to arrest him as publicly as possible to make up for your previous failures?"

Paige did her best to ignore that. She knew that the only way to deal with all of this was to successfully solve the case. Before she and Christopher did that, nothing they said would be good enough for the waiting press.

Julius, of course, had plenty to say. "My name is Julius Bryant! I am a famous author, and these federal agents are arresting me to try to silence my art!"

Paige and Christopher hurried him inside. In there, Paige saw Julius looking around with nearly infinite curiosity as they marched him through to the interrogation room.

"All of this is fascinating," he said. "I tried to get access before, of course, but they told me that 'wanting to see it all for a book' wasn't a sufficient reason."

He looked around as if making mental notes of everything he saw there.

"I still don't see why you had to take my laptop from me," he said. "I *demand* my laptop."

He said it with such arrogance, as if he expected Paige and Christopher to do exactly what he said through all of this.

"In here," Christopher replied, taking him into the interrogation room. "Do you want to exercise your right to a lawyer? Do you have a lawyer, or do we need to call for a public defender?"

"I have no need of a lawyer," Julius said. "You have nothing on me, and I have nothing to fear."

Paige wasn't convinced by that. As far as she could see from the evidence they had on him, Julius had plenty to fear.

"Are you *sure* that you don't want a lawyer?"

"I can represent myself better than any mere lawyer can!"

Paige raised an eyebrow at that. In the absence of a psych evaluation saying he wasn't competent to make the decision, Julius had the right to refuse counsel if he wished, but it would make their jobs more delicate. Paige had no wish to see anything they got from him thrown out of court.

She gestured for Christopher to talk to her out of the room. Julius made to follow them.

"You stay here," Christopher said.

"But how am I meant to write all of it then?" Julius demanded. "No, that simply won't…"

Christopher shut the door to the interrogation room, locking him inside.

"You're worried about whether we can interview him," Christopher guessed.

Paige nodded. "If he's delusional, then interrogating him without a lawyer present might get all the evidence thrown out of court."

"*Is* he delusional?" Christopher asked. "As far as I can see, he's utterly narcissistic, but he's aware of what's happening around him, intelligent, even manipulative."

Paige had to admit that he had a point.

"All right," she said. "And he has explicitly turned down a lawyer, but if he shows signs of not understanding what's going on, we'll have to stop."

Christopher nodded. "Let's just hope that in the meantime, we can get him to admit to what he's done."

"How are we going to approach this?" Paige asked.

"I'll have the techs go through his computer for any evidence. He doesn't seem to have this misericord dagger on him, so we'll send a search team to his house to toss it and try to find it. In the meantime, we'll just talk to him, see if he's prepared to admit anything. He seems to want to talk, so let's see if he's willing to talk about what he's done."

Paige followed as Christopher led the way back into the interrogation room. Julius was there, and looking pretty irate.

"How dare you cut me out like that? How am I meant to write all of this if you won't allow me to see crucial parts of it?"

117

"Mr. Bryant, our focus isn't on making it easy for you to write a book; it's on trying to catch a murderer," Christopher said. "You understand that we believe *you* are that murderer?"

"Based on what?" Julius demanded.

Paige was starting to worry again about all of this, and not just because anything Julius said might or might not be admissible. He was so grandiose and arrogant that it was going to take real work to get anything out of him.

"Based on what you wrote," Paige said. "Your serial novel is written as if you are claiming to have committed all of the murders. You include details of the murders of Gisele Newbury, Meredith Park, and Peggy Cane."

"I can write what I wish!" Julius replied. "I will not be held back by your petty morality around such things."

"And does not being held back by morality extend to committing murder?" Christopher asked.

"Is *this* how the FBI interrogates someone?" Julius countered. "They just ask them over and over again if they did it? Honestly, I could write far better. I *will* write far better, once you return my laptop."

"You'll get it back once our tech teams have been through it to look for evidence," Christopher said. "But you could save us all some time if you tell us whether they'll find anything incriminating in there."

"Why would I save you time?" Julius asked. "I am getting more than enough out of being here. Scenes that will help my work and plenty of free publicity. At last, the press will give me the attention I deserve."

Paige tried to think of a question that would actually get him to engage. That was the hardest part of all of this, trying to get him to actually talk to them, rather than going off on his own tangent.

"And what attention is it that you think they should give you, Julius?" Paige asked. "What should they remember you for?"

"For being the greatest writer in the world today, of course!" he replied. "For pushing literary boundaries that others dare not push!"

Paige had half hoped that he would talk about wanting notoriety, or even come out and lay claim to his crimes. She knew that he had plenty of reasons not to admit to murder, but even so, it seemed a little strange that someone who had killed for what seemed like narcissistic reasons would be so reticent on that aspect.

"Tell me about Meredith Park," Paige said.

"The second victim?" Julius's attention seemed to have been caught again. "She was a most fascinating woman. Beautiful, of course, but I was more interested in the attention that so many people gave to her. People watched her, and she was always so *nice*."

"*You* watched her, didn't you, Julius?" Paige asked.

"Me?"

Christopher jumped in then. "We have footage of you from the restaurant at the Renaissance Faire, staring straight at her shortly before her death."

"Like I said, I found her fascinating. Of course I stared at her," Julius said. "She was... there was something about her that even I found it hard to pin down with words."

He said that as if it meant that no one could have caught that part about her, because surely if he couldn't, it was impossible.

What interested Paige was that he was so prepared to admit that he'd been there. It didn't seem to occur to him that this tied him to the murder, or maybe he was just confident that he could stop Paige and Christopher from truly linking him to the murder.

"What about Gisele Newbury?" Christopher asked. "Have you ever met her?"

Julius shrugged. It wasn't an answer, not really.

"We're going to pull traffic cam footage for your car," Christopher said. "We'll know if you were on the same route as her. We'll know if you had a chance to run into her."

"A valid way of investigating the lead," Julius said. "Although personally, I would have my characters pull up the GPS for my car, so that they would know the location much more accurately."

"Julius," Paige said. "You need to take this more seriously. You've been arrested on suspicion of murder."

"Ah, *you're* going to play the sympathetic one, probably the one who has insights into the personality of the suspect," Julius said. "Well then, what do you make of me, Agent King?"

Paige wondered how much to say. The goal here wasn't simply to diagnose Julius; it was to get him to talk. Her private thought was that Julius was deeply narcissistic, and clearly thought that he was in charge of the entire situation. She suspected, though, that if she said that, it wouldn't help to get any answers out of him.

"I think that you're obviously clever," Paige said. "I also think that you're playing games with us. Why aren't you answering our questions directly?"

"It's more fun this way," Julius said. "What's it like, being an FBI agent? Especially as a woman. I imagine that there must be all kinds of complications. Especially with your background. What was it like seeing your father killed? What was it like, when your mother moved in with a new husband, only for him to assault you?"

Paige felt a wave of anger rising in her. She knew that Julius was doing it deliberately, but it was still hard to hold back from lunging forward to strike at him.

Christopher seemed to sense the problem, stepping in to interrupt before Paige could act.

"I'm more interested in where you were when Gisele Newbury was killed, and when Peggy Cane was murdered," he said. "I know you know the exact times, because you wrote about the murders in such detail."

"I did, didn't I?" Julius said, seeming proud, but not actually answering the question.

"Where were you?" Christopher asked.

"Oh... somewhere." Julius had a cunning look on his face, but Paige couldn't tell if it was because he thought he was getting away with murder, or just because he was playing games with the FBI.

"Where, exactly?" Christopher insisted.

"I don't remember. Writing is hard."

"You don't remember?" Paige asked.

Julius shrugged, and Paige headed for the door.

"Where are you going?" he demanded.

Paige stopped. "Tell me about Peggy. Tell me how you knew about her murder."

"Such a fascinating case," Julius said. "Such a fascinating woman. The way she died there in the locker room. It's almost like a locked room mystery."

Paige had put up with enough from the writer. She headed for the door, Christopher following in her wake.

"It's him," Christopher said. "It has to be. No alibi, writing about the murders in detail. Obviously a narcissist. It's him."

Paige thought about it. There was a lot of circumstantial evidence stacking up around Julius, yet... where was the misericord? Where was the direct evidence linking him to the crime?

More than that, Paige found herself thinking about the kind of man who had committed these crimes. The kind of man who had lashed out because of small insults. Was that man Julius?

Paige just wasn't sure. There was something wrong here, something that didn't quite fit. Paige couldn't quite put her finger on it, because at first glance it appeared that all the evidence they had pointed one way, but still…

"I don't think that Julius Bryant is the killer."

CHAPTER TWENTY ONE

Paige saw Christopher staring at her in something like disbelief.

"You don't think that Bryant is the killer?" he said.

Paige could only shake her head. The feeling wouldn't go away, no matter how much she told herself that the evidence pointed his way.

"There are things that don't fit," Paige said.

"He literally wrote about how he killed these three women, Paige," Christopher said.

"So he's a bad writer who uses the deaths of innocent women to improve his profile," Paige replied. "I'm not sure that it means that he's the killer. In fact, it's part of what's persuading me that he isn't."

Christopher frowned. It was hard to ignore how good looking he was when his brow furrowed like that. Paige knew that she couldn't focus on that, though.

"The fact that he's written something close to a confession is evidence that he's *not* the killer?" Christopher said, apparently not quite believing it even as he said it.

Paige did her best to explain. "My point is that throughout all of this, he has looked at all of it like a writer. Everything is material for his next book. *Everything.* He's obsessive about the writing, but when we talked about the women, all he could say was how fascinating they were. That's not the pathology of our killer."

"Unless he's killing these women just to provide more material for his books?" Christopher suggested. "I mean, you have to admit that he might be capable of doing something like that. And he's obviously a narcissist."

"He is," Paige agreed.

"So it could be him?"

Paige considered it. Was it possible that she'd just misunderstood the motivations of the killer? Was it possible that all of this wasn't about some lethally offended narcissist, but about one who considered his pet writing project to be more important than the lives of the women he killed?

"No," Paige said at last. "Think about the footage from the bus. Think about the way Gisele was making people angry with her driving.

We see our guy getting into an altercation with Peggy Cane. This is about revenge for insults, and Julius Bryant isn't interested in that."

"What if you're wrong?" Christopher asked. "We can't just let a guy go just because your hunch says that he isn't the killer."

"We've been here before," Paige pointed out. In previous cases, there had been moments when they'd had a suspect in custody, and Christopher hadn't been willing to believe that he wasn't their man.

"What if this is the time when we really do have the killer?" Christopher asked. "All the evidence we have…"

"Is circumstantial," Paige said. "Where is the physical evidence? Where is the murder weapon?"

Christopher looked as if he didn't understand. "Like I told Julius, I've sent a forensic team to his house."

"But the killer doesn't keep the weapon in his house, does he?" Paige pointed out. "Look at what happened with Peggy Cane. He argued with her on the bus. Then, shortly after she got off at the bus station, she was found dead. The killer didn't run home to get his misericord. He had to have it on him, ready to use. He carries it around with him."

"Maybe today's the day when Julius decided to leave it at home," Christopher suggested, but he didn't sound as certain as he had before. "Maybe he only carries it with him when he's actively out looking for someone to kill."

That was possible, but for Paige, it still didn't fit with her profile of the killer. This was an opportunistic killer, who reacted to the petty insults of ordinary life. This was someone who had to be ready to strike back at a moment's notice.

"I'm not even sure his coat is right," Paige said. "Yes, he has a long coat, but look at it, and then look at the footage from the bus. I'm pretty sure it's a different design."

"He might own more than one coat," Christopher pointed out.

"So a different coat, and he's not carrying the murder weapon, and he's not reacting the way we think he ought to? He isn't even getting angry with us in there, except at the thought of being left out of all of this. I'm telling you, Christopher, this isn't our guy."

"So we just happen to have found another narcissist who was staring at Meredith Park shortly before she was murdered?"

That was a more damning piece of the puzzle, but it was still circumstantial.

"*Everyone* paid her attention," Paige said. "And I don't think it's a coincidence. I want to go back through Julius's posts. I want to check the dates on them."

She heard Christopher sigh. "All right. I trust you, Paige. If there are things that you need to check, then check them, but I need to go back in there to try to get a confession out of Bryant. You know that we can't afford to just ignore someone who is this strong a suspect."

Paige understood what he was saying. With the pressure from the press, if they just let him go on her hunch, there would be instant anger from Agent Sauer, demanding to know what they were doing. There was a chance that they would even be replaced on the case.

"I know you have to keep going with him," Paige said. "Just... don't push too hard, or I get the feeling he might tell you what you want to hear, just for the attention."

"I'll be careful," Christopher said, and headed back into the interrogation room.

Paige went to the office she and Christopher had borrowed there in the field office. She started up her laptop and began to look for discrepancies. She checked the footage taken from the bus station first. Sure enough, while the figure there arguing with Peggy Cane wore a long coat, it didn't look anything like the one that Julius Bryant had with him.

Christopher had already made the obvious counterargument to that point though. Paige needed to find more if she was going to convince her partner that they had the wrong man.

She looked at Julius's serial novel next. Crucially, Paige was looking for the upload dates of each section. If the Gisele Newbury section had been uploaded on the day of her murder, then yes, it seemed like an incredible coincidence that Julius had happened to be in the restaurant of the Renaissance Faire just before Meredith Park died. But there was another possibility, one that Paige quickly found borne out by the dates on the uploads.

In that moment, Paige thought that she understood Julius Bryant's involvement. She hurried over to the interrogation room, where Christopher was still trying to get an increasingly agitated looking Julius Bryant to talk to him.

"It all started with Meredith, didn't it Julius?" Paige said, as she stepped into the room.

"What?" Christopher said. "Paige, the first victim was-"

"I know Gisele Newbury was the killer's first victim, but for Julius, it started with Meredith Park. I just checked the dates on your work, Julius. The first post was on the day of Meredith's murder. You wrote her murder first, then wrote Gisele's afterwards."

"Did you like my work?" Julius asked. Even here, even now, he was looking for validation?

"I'm mostly interested in where you got your ideas," Paige said.

"Ah, the question every author gets asked."

"*My* theory is that you were obsessed with Meredith Park. I think if we look back further through the security footage from the restaurant, we'll find you there, again and again, looking her way. I think that when she was killed, you felt like you had to write it, as… what? Some kind of tribute?"

"Can a tribute bring the loveliest of flowers back to life?" Julius said. "In his sonnets, Shakespeare writes of keeping his love alive through verse. It's a lie, but I had to try. I had to. I *have* to."

Paige turned her attention to Christopher. "He only wrote the Gisele Newbury section after Meredith's death. My guess is, once he'd written the part for her, once he'd gotten some attention for it, he felt like he had to keep going."

"A work is not complete until the audience deems it so!" Julius said.

"It doesn't mean he didn't do this," Christopher said. "He might have killed Gisele, killed Meredith, and only then decided to write about it."

"I thought you said that you thought he was killing them specifically to have something to write about?" Paige pointed out.

"Does this mean that I'm free to go?" Julius said. He stood and started for the door.

"No, it doesn't," Christopher said. He gestured for Paige to speak to him outside again. Once they were outside the door to the interrogation room once more, he looked a little less certain than he had, though.

"You still think it's him?" Paige asked.

"I still think it's possible," Christopher said. "We can hold him for 24 hours. We'll see what results come in from the search of his house and from looking back through the security footage. But let's say for a moment that you're right, and Julius Bryant isn't the killer. Now what?"

That was the question that was bugging Paige because she didn't have an answer right then.

"I'm not sure," she admitted.

"We need something more than that, Paige," Christopher said. "It's not just that Sauer is going to be breathing down my neck for the number of arrests we've made that haven't proved to be the killer, it's that the whole FBI is going to start to look bad in the eyes of the Kentucky press. They're all clustered downstairs still, waiting for a comment that we can't give them in the middle of an active investigation. I thought we were going to be able to announce that we had the killer in custody, but now, they'll be happy to run more stories about how we aren't doing our jobs while women are dying. And honestly, I'm not sure they're wrong."

Paige could feel the weight of the pressure there, not least because it was on her just as much as Christopher. They needed an idea that would get them to the killer. The physical evidence wasn't taking them anywhere. Paige needed to go deeper into her profile of the killer. She needed to think about the ways Nadia and Julius had reacted.

She needed to think about what made this killer unique, too. This was an individual, not just a general profile. They knew a few specific things about him. They'd *seen* specific things about his behavior. This wasn't just a delusional narcissist like Julius, obsessed with his own brilliance but ultimately more fascinated by women than a danger to them.

Nor was this man quite like Nadia, who had a history of violence, but who mostly seemed to be about grabbing attention. The killer had been deliberately cryptic in his efforts, not claiming credit the way Paige had assumed that he would.

No, the defining factor was the sense of insult. Gisele Newbury had been a driver who upset people. Peggy Cane had clearly argued with him on the bus. Meredith... well, everyone said that she was nice to everyone, but how many opportunities for unintentionally slighting someone did working in a restaurant offer? Plenty, if she was in a rush, and didn't pay someone the attention they thought they deserved.

This was a man who rose to any insult, no matter how small, with deadly force. That meant that he was potentially a man who could be provoked into action, baited into a response. If Paige judged what that response was going to be, then they might have a chance to stop him before anyone else died.

Paige looked out of the window at the waiting crowd of journalists.

"I have an idea that might catch the killer," she said. "There's only one problem with it."

"What's that?" Christopher asked, looking suddenly both hopeful and worried.

"I really don't think you're going to like it."

CHAPTER TWENTY TWO

Paige hurried down through the FBI field office, heading for the waiting press with a sense of trepidation. What she was about to do could put her life at risk.

"I'm really not sure this is a good idea," Christopher said.

"It's our best chance of trying to catch the killer," Paige replied. "We provoke him to strike on our terms."

"By trying to kill *you*," Christopher pointed out. It was clear that he didn't like any of this. Was that just concern for his partner, or did Paige dare to believe that there might be something more to it than that?

"But I can handle myself," Paige said, "and we'll be ready and waiting for him. Trust me, Christopher, this is our best shot."

"Sauer isn't going to like you putting yourself in harm's way like this."

Paige forced herself to shrug it off like it was nothing, when in fact it meant a great deal that her boss was going to be angry about this. Agent Sauer had been the one to give her a job at the BAU, and he was ultimately the one who would determine if she got to work on the Exsanguination Killer case. The last thing Paige wanted to do was get into his bad books over this.

"So don't tell him," Paige said.

"You know I have to, Paige." Even as he said it, Christopher moved to make the call. Was he hoping that if he got Agent Sauer involved, he might be able to stop Paige from putting herself at risk?

Paige appreciated the concern, but if she didn't do this, didn't lure the killer to them, Paige wasn't sure how they were going to catch him before he killed someone else. Maybe there was something in the evidence that they could follow, some trace that they could run down that would lead back to him, but the sheer time it would take would give the killer too many opportunities to strike again.

Paige had to do this, had to try to bring him to them. She was confident that it would work, too. Everything about this killer's pathology said that he would have no choice once he heard her; he would have to do his best to try to kill her.

She kept heading downstairs, towards the waiting press corps. While she did it, she could hear Christopher on his phone behind her, obviously talking to Sauer. Paige walked a little quicker. She knew that Christopher had to make their boss aware of something like this; she even appreciated that he was trying to find a way to protect her, but she couldn't let him stop her.

Paige made it downstairs, into the main lobby of the field office. She was halfway across it when her phone went off. It was Sauer. Paige ignored the call, knowing that if she answered there was a good chance that he might order her not to do this. She suspected that he wouldn't like the idea of one of his agents using herself as bait for a killer, and once he gave her a direct order, Paige would be caught in an invidious position: go along with that order and leave a killer free to murder more women, or go against it and risk losing her job.

At least this way, Paige could pretend that she'd been too busy with the press conference she was about to give to answer.

Her phone went off again, with a text this time.

Agent King, what you're planning to do is foolish in the extreme. Don't do something that could endanger your life and those of others.

That was enough to make Paige pause, but not to make her stop. She knew what it was like for the families who lost a loved one to a killer, and for the people who found a body. She knew better than anyone the waves of impact killers could cause, rippling out beyond their victim, to everyone that person knew, everyone who had met them. Even Julius Bryant, in his way, was only acting as he was because of this killer.

Paige knew the empty, horrified feeling of looking down at the dead. She knew the pain of a family torn apart by death. Paige would risk her own life without hesitation if it meant that she could stop anyone else from feeling the way she had felt as a girl. And if that meant ignoring her boss now, so be it.

Paige stepped out from the FBI field office, and instantly, the press were there around her, cameras raised, microphones extended. Their questions came out thick and fast.

"Agent King, what do you say to the protesters outside the online creators conference who want Julius Bryant released?"

"What assurances can you give the people of Lexington that no more women will be murdered?"

"Do you think you're the right person to investigate killers, given your history?"

Paige bit back the urge to retort. She knew that was what the reporters wanted. They wanted anything that would show her as incompetent or unstable, to fit with the story that the FBI had no place in Lexington, investigating these killings. Paige knew that she had to appear calm, confident, and in control if she was going to make this work.

It didn't matter if she was angry about the questions, or if she was afraid about the potential consequences of what she was about to do. All that mattered was that Paige's best chance to stop this killer was to lure him out.

Paige took a moment to get her hotel room key out, holding it loosely in her hand, moving it back and forth as if to deal with the stress of being asked so many questions so quickly with the cameras pointing at her.

"Ok," she said. "If all of you will step back, I'm prepared to talk to you about the current progress of the case, and our latest theories on the killer, but I need you to give me some space."

It was about the only thing Paige could have said that would get the press to give Paige the space she needed, and probably the only thing that could hold their attention long enough to do what she had to do.

"Now," Paige said, as the press backed away. "We have Julius Bryant in custody, but we are no longer convinced that he is the killer. We plan on releasing him as soon as confirmation of his alibi comes through. The real killer is still out there."

Just on its own, that was likely to get Paige into trouble, when Julius hadn't been released yet.

"So does this mean that you aren't making any progress on the case?" one of the reporters asked.

"On the contrary, we believe that we are very close to catching the killer," Paige said, still moving the key in her hand in a semi-conscious movement to deal with the stress.

"They say that you're a profiler," a reporter called out. "That you have a Ph.D. in understanding the criminal mind. Why haven't you profiled this killer, Agent King?"

This was Paige's moment. "Because there's nothing special to say about this individual."

"Nothing special?" one of the reporters said. "What about the fleur-de-lis? They're saying that this killer is elegant, that he kills with particular style."

"Who says that?" Paige countered. "The last thing this killer manages to be is *stylish*. He's ordinary, run of the mill. He walks up to people and stabs them. There's nothing special about that."

"So you really don't think that there's anything special about this killer?" another of the reporters asked.

"Nothing special about him at all," Paige said. "If anything, he's kind of pathetic."

"So why has he managed to evade the FBI for so long?"

Paige took a breath, knowing that each thing she said put her in more danger, but also knowing that she had to push this as far as she dared if she was going to get a reaction from the killer.

"Luck. Nothing but luck. Let's not pretend that this is a clever man, or one with a particular flare for this. I'm frankly astonished that you're all here. This is someone who is barely worthy of your time, and certainly not worthy of anyone's respect. He'll be caught soon, and once he is, no one will even remember him."

Paige stared down the nearest camera in a challenge as she said it. She made herself laugh then, even though her fear made it hard to do.

"Seriously. This is nobody. A pathetic little nobody."

She turned and went back inside then. Christopher was waiting for her, his expression grave.

"Sauer wants to speak to you, now," he said. It was obvious that saying no wasn't an option. "This is bad, Paige. He's angry. Really angry."

Christopher led the way up to the office, where the image of Agent Sauer was there on the screen. As Christopher had said, he didn't look happy. In fact, he looked as if he might shout at Paige at any moment.

"What do you think you were just doing, Agent King?" he demanded. "I just watched your little press conference. In it, you just antagonized a serial killer to the point where he's likely to kill again, just to spite you. Do you have any *idea* of the damage you've just done?"

"The idea was to bait the serial killer in," Paige said. She held up the keys she'd been holding throughout the press conference. "He knows where I will be now. He'll think working it out proves how clever he is. I'm willing to bet that he's not going to lash out randomly. He comes for people who have insulted him. He's going to try to kill *me*."

"And that's meant to make things *better*?" Agent Sauer demanded, his voice rising. "Give me one reason why I shouldn't call you back to Quantico and fire you right now, Agent King."

Horror filled Paige at the prospect that he might do just that. If she lost her job, she would never be in a position to learn more about the killer who had haunted her since the day he'd killed her father. Paige had worked so hard to get where she was, and now, it sounded as though she might be about to lose it all.

"I agree with Agent King, sir," Christopher said.

Agent Sauer turned his gaze Christopher's way. "You were the one who called me about your concerns, Agent Marriott."

"I have concerns for Paige's safety," Christopher said. "But I also agree that if the killer is still out there, this is the best way to catch him. Paige has been right in her assessments of killers before. I trust her now."

"And are you willing to bet your job with the BAU on this too, Marriott?" Sauer demanded. "Because that's what it means if all of this goes wrong. If the killer strikes elsewhere, if he murders some other woman… the FBI will have to give this case over to the local PD, and I will see to it that both of you are posted to minor field offices, if you keep your jobs at all."

Paige's heart was in her mouth. She couldn't let Christopher take that kind of risk with a career he'd built up over years.

"I trust Paige's judgement," Christopher said.

"So be it," Sauer replied, and hung up.

Paige felt sick. She couldn't believe what had just happened.

"Christopher," she said. "You didn't have to do that, not for me."

"I think Sauer would have gotten you on the first flight back to Quantico if I didn't," Christopher said. "And while I don't know if you're right, if you are, then we can't afford to just sit back and wait for this killer to murder someone else. But we do this right, Paige. You've tried to lure a killer into a trap. Now, we need to make sure that it's one he can't escape from."

CHAPTER TWENTY THREE

He was sitting at home, watching the news, watching the impact that he was having on the world while he contemplated what he was going to do next. The sounds of his apartment block surrounded him, the music of the woman on the floor above proving far too annoying, as usual.

He wanted to just walk up there and kill her. He'd been thinking about it for a while now. Ever since his mother had died and he'd gone off the medication the doctors had tried to force on him to control him. She hadn't insulted him directly yet, hadn't turned him down like Meredith Park, cursed at him like Peggy Cane, or almost run him over like Giselle Newbury, but that small annoyance certainly felt like it could be a reason to pick her.

It would be easy to engineer it, the way duelists had done for centuries. He could walk up to her door and tell her to turn her music off. He had no doubt that she would tell him to go away in the bluntest terms possible. After that… well, justice would be required.

Just not here, not now. He would have to pick a place and a time when it couldn't just be traced back to him. The same way that he'd held off on killing Meredith and Peggy until there had been a chance to do it without being seen. Lesser people, with their lesser morality, didn't understand what he was doing. They would call him a criminal, a murderer, if they realized that it was him. Their petty courts would try to convict him, as if he didn't stand above all of that.

So he sat in his apartment, trying to think of a way and a place.

The apartment was… not what he deserved. It was too small, too dingy. There was a damp patch on one of the walls, and the reception on the TV flickered every so often as the cable messed up. He had to sit in a slightly worn red felt armchair, rather than the throne he deserved. His collection of medieval oddments, and his stack of fleur-de-lis ornaments, had to sit on slightly rickety shelves. Even the manager of the building was getting onto him about his rent, as if such things mattered to him.

Briefly, he thought about dueling the building manager, but no, there was something more satisfying somehow when it was a woman. It wasn't that he was afraid of the manager. That wasn't it. It didn't matter at all that he was three hundred pounds and a former boxer. It didn't. It was just… better when it was a woman, someone who should show him respect and adoration, rather than insulting him.

Which left him contemplating where best to kill his upstairs neighbor while he watched the news.

The news had been good, the last couple of days. So much of it had been devoted to him. People had spoken about him with fear and awe. Experts had been called onto news shows to talk about him and guess at his motivations. They'd always gotten it wrong, which annoyed him slightly, but at least they talked about the cleverness and precision of what he did.

There was even a guy writing a book about him. He'd been quite surprised to find that the guy in question had been arrested for the murders but maybe that was as it should be. Someone who worshipped him that much should be willing to take the fall for him, at least temporarily.

He assumed that the next time he killed, Julius Bryant would be released. Then he would be even more grateful, and would write even better things about him.

Everything was going well, until the FBI agent came out to speak.

He'd been watching Agent King since she arrived on the case. He thought that it was amusing to have a pretty young woman trying to catch him, as if she'd ever get close. He found himself oscillating between dislike of the fact that she was trying to catch him, and feeling flattered that the FBI was putting so much effort into chasing him.

He'd heard from the news that she was an expert on killers in her own right, and that she'd even lost her father to a serial killer. If there was anyone out there who could, who *should,* appreciate him and be appropriately scared, then it was her.

Then she stepped out in front of the FBI building and started to speak.

"There's nothing special to say about this individual."

That was the first sign that something was wrong, but it only got worse as she kept talking. She insulted him, over and over, belittling him, saying that he wasn't special, wasn't smart. When she said that he was someone who was barely worthy of the FBI's time, he felt like his blood was boiling.

He leapt up in one movement, snatching his misericord off the shelf where he kept it and grabbing his long coat. He didn't have enough time to search around for his hat, because he was too busy running towards the door. Agent King thought that he wasn't smart, wasn't special?

Well, with those words, she'd signed her own death warrant. He forgot all about his neighbor in that moment. She didn't matter anymore, the small insults of everyday life fading before the kind of grand challenges to everything he was doing that Agent King had thrown out. Such things were unforgivable.

She thought she was safe because she was a federal agent? She wasn't. When he killed her, the news would have to say again that he was special, that he was dangerous. They would all shout about how he had punished the agent who had dared to insult him.

Agent Paige King didn't think he was smart? Didn't think he could get to her? Well, he was smarter than she thought. He'd worked out *exactly* where to go to get to her.

CHAPTER TWENTY FOUR

It took more work to plan an ambush than Paige had thought. She'd imagined that she and Christopher could just go back to their hotel, sit there, and wait for the killer to arrive, but apparently, it didn't work like that.

"First thing's first," Christopher said. "You'll wear a tactical vest at all times at the hotel, right?"

"If it's obvious, then the killer will know that I'm expecting him," Paige replied. "He'll only come for me if he doesn't expect the trap."

"So wear the tactical vest under your jacket," Christopher said, "but there's no way that you're going to that hotel again without one. This is a killer who likes a single thrust to the heart. Your vest will stop that first blow, if we're too slow spotting him."

"We won't be," Paige insisted. "We know where he's going to come. We know what room. So you and I go there and wait, and the moment he tries to get me to come to the door so he can stab me, we'll be ready to pounce."

Christopher shook his head, though. "That's not enough of a plan, Paige. Sure, we *might* be able to arrest him like that, but we might also find that he runs the moment he sees us and realizes it's a trap. Or he might be quick to attack you. Or he might lash out at random people in the hotel. Plus, after the way you've done this, Sauer wants the final sign off on the plan. I know him; he'll want a more thorough plan than us both waiting in a room for a bad guy."

Paige couldn't help the feeling that Christopher still didn't like her idea. He'd gone along with it in front of Agent Sauer, but it seemed that had only been to make sure that Paige didn't lose her job there and then.

"You don't think this is a good idea, do you?" Paige asked.

"I think you've put yourself at risk much more than you needed to," Christopher replied. "And while I trust that you've assessed this guy's personality correctly, what if you're wrong? What if he just turns around and starts killing people at random to show that the FBI has no way of stopping him?"

"I don't think that he will," Paige said. "That's not the way he's working. It's about revenge for specific insults, on the person who wronged him. At this point he *has* to kill me."

"That certainty's what I'm worried about," Christopher said. "Because nothing will get you killed quicker in a tactical situation than the belief that you know exactly what's going to happen."

Paige got that, or thought she did. She still wouldn't change what she'd done even if she could.

"This is our best chance of catching him before someone else dies," Paige said. "Maybe our only chance."

"I get that," Christopher said. "But we're meant to be a team, Paige. You can't just go off and make a call this big without including me. That's not what partners do. In one interview, you declared that our main suspect wasn't the killer, and committed us to a dangerous trap that might cost us both our careers if it doesn't cost you your life."

That was the one part of this that Paige felt a trace of guilt for. She'd done this in spite of Christopher's objections, at least partly because she'd wanted to keep him out of any of the trouble that was likely to follow as a result of what she did. She'd assumed that she knew what was needed to close this case, and pretty much forced Christopher into a position where he had to go along with it, risking his job in the process. He was right: that wasn't the kind of thing a good partner did.

Paige had to admit that she was also worried by the risks of all of this. She wasn't stupid; she knew that she'd just baited a man who had killed three women to come and try to kill her. Whatever precautions they took, there was still a possibility that he might succeed.

"You're right," Paige said. "I'm sorry. I just… I thought if it was just me, there wouldn't be any consequences for you if it went wrong."

"That's not how this works," Christopher said. "Partners stick together."

Paige nodded. She'd spent a lot of time worrying that she was getting too close to Christopher, but in some ways, she hadn't even treated him the way she was supposed to as his partner.

"I'm sorry," Paige repeated.

"It's ok," Christopher said. "My main concern now is finding a way to make this work. We'll only get one shot at this. We have to ensure that our guy doesn't have a chance to run, but also that he'll be able to get up to the room without being scared off."

"What's that going to take?" Paige asked.

Christopher sighed. "The first thing we'll need is more bodies. I'll try to get more agents from the field office to help with this, but I might have to reach out to the Lexington PD too and more or less beg them for some plain clothes detectives. We need people to cover the lobby and the stairwells, so that we can stop him if he tries to run. We need to put surveillance in place so that he can't get to the room without us spotting him."

"And then we wait in the room?" Paige asked.

"I'd prefer for us to wait in *my* room," Christopher replied. "If we have the surveillance right, maybe a camera in your room waiting for him, then we can catch him without having to risk him getting a clean run at you. We'll let him go to the room, and we'll be close enough to grab him when he does."

Paige had to admit that it was a much safer plan than the one Paige had come up with, where she and Christopher would just be sitting there when he came for her.

"I'll have to go to the hotel alone, though," Paige said, seeing at least one flaw in this plan. "If he sees me in the middle of a crowd of FBI agents, there's no way that he will attack. He tries to kill women when they're alone."

"I don't like giving him that window of opportunity," Christopher said.

"We can still have people in place," Paige said. "We just have to make it look like... well, like I've just been suspended for giving a press conference I shouldn't have. Like I'm going back to the hotel to collect my things before I go back to D.C."

It was too close to what had almost happened. If Christopher hadn't intervened with Agent Sauer, she might actually have found herself sent home. It was an image that the killer might believe, and an opportunity that he might actually be looking out for.

"We can make that work," Christopher said. "But we need to make sure that everything is set up first. *Don't* go off alone until we're ready. We only get one chance to get this right."

Paige nodded. She understood that part.

"This is going to take a while to set up," Christopher said. "I'll pull together the agents we need, and we'll try to work out the surveillance package that this will require."

It was astonishing, how much work it took to set something like this up. Paige had come up with her plan in a few minutes, but now she had to sit there while Christopher started to make calls to get as many agents as he could for this.

"Paige," he said, "can you go to the local building department's site and try to pull up plans for the hotel?"

"I'm on it," Paige said. She went over to the site and it only took a quick search to find what she needed in the records. The architectural blueprints gave a simple, almost boxlike layout for the hotel, showing all the stairwells and entry points.

"Ok," Christopher said. "We'll need people here, here, and here to cover the entrances. We'll need camera feeds. These stairwells are a potential problem, so we'll need to have a couple of agents to cover them as well."

It seemed as though with every passing minute, the scale of the operation was growing. Paige tried not to think about what other operations the agents they were pulling in for this had been working on, and what crimes might take longer to solve just because of this. Would any criminals get away with what they'd done because this case took priority?

Paige knew that she couldn't think like that. This was about catching a killer. They had to do that, whatever it took.

"Ok," Christopher said. "I think I can get the people we need, and I think Sauer will be on board with it. This is probably your last chance to pull out, Paige."

Paige shook her head. "My chance to pull out of all of this was before I insulted a killer on live television. He's coming for me now; the only question is whether we'll be ready to catch him when he does."

Even if Paige went back to D.C. now, even if she abandoned the case completely, there would still be the risk that the killer was coming for her, that he would follow her just for his chance at revenge. At least this way, they could use that moment to catch him.

"Are you ready to go?" Christopher asked.

Paige nodded. "I'll head back to the hotel in the car now."

"I'll have people tailing you the whole way, and I'll meet you at the hotel," Christopher said. "I'd still rather travel with you."

"He needs to think that I'm alone," Paige replied.

She headed over to the multi-level parking structure that served the field office and several of the surrounding buildings. It was starting to get dark now, with the strip lights around the parking structure casting harsh shadows.

The car was on the second level, and Paige headed up, taking the stairs. It only occurred to her once she was on them that she'd forgotten to grab a tactical vest, the way Christopher wanted. She thought about going back for one just to make him happy, but Paige figured that she could put one on once she reached the hotel. It wouldn't make a difference, and it would look pretty strange if she ran back to the field office now.

Paige headed up to her and Christopher's car, the large black sedan sitting about midway along one row of cars, up next to one of the pillars of concrete that supported the place. Paige clicked on the key to unlock it, trying to think about how things would go at the hotel. She would need to be careful there, especially on the way up to her room. This was a killer who had shown that he liked to hit people on the move in moments of transition, so there was always a chance that he would try to strike while Paige was still on her way to her room.

In that moment, she found herself thinking about Gisele Newbury, found dead on her driveway next to her Porsche, and about Meredith Park, stabbed… as she was going to her car.

Paige's instincts flared a warning as she approached, and she saw a figure step out from behind the pillar next to the car. He was a little over average height, muscular and dark-haired, wearing a long coat over slacks and a t shirt, as if he'd been aiming for some kind of more elegant costume, but had been in too much of a hurry. Paige's eyes were drawn almost automatically to the long, slender, blunt sided dagger that he held in his right hand. A misericord, there to thrust for her heart.

Fear filled Paige as she saw that weapon, and that fear slowed her, stopped her from stepping back and making space to draw her gun the way she should have.

"Time to pay for what you did," he snarled, in a rough voice, and lunged straight at Paige.

CHAPTER TWENTY FIVE

As the killer lunged at her, Paige realized the full extent to which she'd messed up. She'd assumed that by giving him a piece of information about where she was going to be, she could control where he was going to come for her. Now, though, she realized that she'd made the killer so angry that he hadn't wanted to wait even that long, and it hadn't bothered him coming this close to the FBI field office because he simply couldn't conceive of anyone capturing him.

Which meant that now, instead of him walking into Paige's trap, she'd walked into his.

For an instant, terror rooted Paige to the spot, but then instinct took over and she twisted to one side, the misericord only nicking her side rather than thrusting through her heart.

"Die!" the killer snarled, slamming into her, his greater size and weight slamming Paige back into the concrete pillar, the impact knocking the breath out of her. "You think you can insult me and not pay the price?"

His arm went back to stab again and Paige grabbed for it, managing to get one hand on his arm, while the other went onto the blade. The square sides meant that it didn't slice open her entire hand the way a normal blade might have, but it still took all of Paige's strength to hold on.

She snapped her head forward to strike her assailant on the bridge of his nose. The pain of that made him rear back, buying Paige some space, but also meant that he ripped the knife out of her grip, the tip of it cutting her hand on the way out. *That* part at least was razor sharp.

Paige pushed away from him, not trying to move his weight so much as move herself, like a swimmer pushing off the side of a pool. Paige got a little distance, and worked to create more. Against a knife, space was her friend.

The killer seemed to sense that, coming at her fast. Paige darted between two cars, then leapt over the hood of a Camaro, hoping that she was faster, even if she didn't have the size or strength advantage in this encounter.

The slide over the hood bought Paige a second or two. That gave her enough time to draw her Glock, turning to try to bring it on target. She managed to get off a shot, but it went wide, shattering the window of a car and setting off its alarm. Perhaps that would bring help, but Paige doubted it. She was alone for this.

The killer slammed into Paige again, and this time the two of them slammed into the ground. The impact jarred the gun from Paige's hand, sending it spinning away under a nearby car. Paige started to reach for it, but then the knife was coming down towards her head, and Paige had to buck and roll, kicking the killer off her to avoid it.

She got to her feet, and he was in front of her, the knife held casually.

"I don't think we've been formally introduced," Paige said. "I'm Agent Paige King, and you are?"

Mostly, Paige said it to buy herself some time in which to think, but a part of her suspected that she might actually get an answer. This was a man who thought of himself as more important than anyone else, as *better* than anyone else. He was also someone who'd adopted something curiously medieval in the symbology of his crimes, and who attacked people for insults. Perhaps old fashioned manners would come into this.

"Damian Carr," he replied. "Although you can call me 'my lord'."

Paige ignored that. Damian here had already decided that he was going to kill her; being obsequious to him wouldn't change that.

"Why the focus on the medieval, Damian?" she asked. "What is it about that time that fascinates you so much?"

"I discovered my link to those times some years ago," Damian said. "My family is old, and royal by blood. My mother checked. She boasted about it so much. Even kept the fleur-de-lis that was our symbol around our home. And rightly so."

"So you adopted it," Paige said.

"It is mine by right! It was a time when a man of the right blood and breeding would be treated with honor," Damian said. "When someone like you would not have been permitted to speak out of turn about me. Those who lapsed in their courtesy dueled for it, and died."

"I did that to lure you in," Paige said. "You're trapped here, Damian."

It was a lie, but Paige hoped that it was a useful one. If Damian believed that more FBI agents were about to pile into the parking structure, then there was a chance that he would make a run for it. Now

142

that Paige knew his name, she and Christopher could put out an APB for him and track him down if he did.

"No," Damian said. "I don't think so. And I told you to call me 'my lord'!"

He lunged at her with the knife again. Paige dodged around a car, then kicked out at his knee as he came forward. She felt the impact jar his knee, but it didn't break, and Damian cut down, the point of his misericord cutting into her leg before Paige jerked it back.

He ran at her once more and Paige stepped to the side, grabbing him and slamming him headfirst into a car's windshield. Another alarm blared, but Paige was more interested in the part where she had a brief moment in which to try to overpower Damian. She grabbed his knife arm, trying to twist it behind his back, but he was too strong, he wrenched his arm free and slashed with the knife. If he'd used a different weapon, the wound as it slashed into Paige's shoulder would have been terrible, but the blunt edges of the misericord meant that it only hit her with bruising force.

Paige went stumbling to the floor and Damian came at her again. Paige rolled out of the way of his first knife blow, then kicked up, catching him in the face. He fell back now, but quickly stood with a roar of pain, charging at her again before Paige could even start to stand.

Paige was starting to realize that she couldn't take down this suspect head on. She certainly couldn't do it while she was lying on her back, with a knife descending towards her head.

Fear sent Paige rolling underneath a pickup truck, the misericord slamming into the asphalt right where her head had been. Paige scrambled away under the next car, trying to find some measure of safety in movement, hiding from the killer as he stalked her.

"You can't hide for long," Damian said. "I'll find you, and I'll kill you. It's what you deserve. It's what's *going* to happen."

He clearly couldn't imagine a world in which he didn't get his way. Paige was determined to stop him, though, and she continued to make her way under the cars, playing cat and mouse with him, determined to keep out of sight. In this environment, her smaller size was an advantage, but Paige still had to be careful. If she came out from under the wrong car, she might find Damian already in front of her, knife coming down to kill her.

Paige needed something that would equalize this, and she thought she saw what she needed a few cars over. Her gun lay there beneath the car she and Christopher had been using. If Paige could just get to it, she had a chance to end this.

Paige started to crawl on her stomach, trying to move quickly but silently in the cramped confines of the space underneath the cars. It was like going under the netting on the FBI's obstacle course back in training, only there hadn't been a serial killer waiting if she'd gotten it wrong, only her instructors.

Paige kept going, ignoring the way her back scraped on the underside of the cars. It didn't matter if she lost a little skin getting through if she could only reach her weapon. One more car and she would be there.

In that moment, Paige heard a sound behind her, and felt something grab her ankle. She looked back to see Damian there, crouched by the car with his misericord, trying to drag her out.

Paige kicked at his hand desperately, once, then again. On the third try, his grip broke, letting her shoot forward from under the car and grab for her waiting Glock. Paige came up with it triumphantly, looking around for the killer. Now, they were playing a very different game of cat and mouse, one where *she* had the advantage.

"Come out, Damian," she said. "It's over."

The problem was that, for a narcissist like him, it wouldn't be over. He'd still think that he had a chance here, that everything would work out his way in the end. Was Paige going to have to shoot him to stop him?

Paige hoped that it wouldn't come to that, but she also knew that she couldn't afford to hesitate if he came at her with that blade again. He'd already shown how dangerous he was with it, and Paige had the wounds to prove it. She made her way around the cars, trying to clear the space between each pair of them before she moved on to the next. In an environment like this, though, with so much cover, the truth was that Damian could be anywhere.

Paige could think of one easy way to get him to show himself, though.

"What's wrong, Damian? You can't be afraid, can you? You know you're better than me, so why not come out and prove it?"

Taunting him had gotten her into all of this, but maybe it could also get Paige out of it too. Would Damian be able to resist coming out to try to take her on directly? She found herself thinking about another word he'd used. He'd said that people who lapsed in courtesy dueled for it. Was that what he thought this was?

144

"This isn't how you duel," Paige said. "You don't sneak up on your opponent. That's not honorable. That's cowardice. Come out. Show yourself."

Paige fully expected that to bring him roaring out from behind one of the cars towards her. She was so primed for it that when she heard one of the doors there in the parking facility open, Paige spun towards it with her gun raised.

She found herself looking at Christopher, standing there holding a tactical vest in one hand.

"Paige?" he said with a frown. "What is it? I came by to tell you that you've forgotten your tactical vest, but... what is all this?"

"The killer is here somewhere," Paige said. "He's... look out!"

Too late, Paige spotted the movement from behind one of the cars nearest the doors, obviously where Damian had been trying to work his way to an exit. Now, though, he wasn't trying to leave. He rushed at Christopher, and in that moment, Christopher simply had no time in which to react. Damian was on him before he could do anything, grabbing him and moving behind him in one smooth movement, an arm going around Christopher's throat.

He set the point of the misericord against Christopher's eye, so close that the least movement would be enough to drive it home, all the way into Christopher's brain. Damian would be able to kill him before either Christopher or Paige could react.

He smiled in something like triumph, his eyes locked on Paige.

"And so we have the other half of the pair hunting for me, defeated easily. Now, Agent King, you are going to do exactly what I say, or your partner here is going to die."

CHAPTER TWENTY SIX

Paige stood there covering Damian, feeling the rush of fear through her at the fact that he had Christopher there in his control like that. The idea of him being killed was a horrifying one, and one that Paige couldn't accept; she wouldn't allow it. She would do whatever it took to keep Christopher safe.

"Put the weapon down and we can talk about this, Damian," she said. "We can take you in, and there will be a trial, where everyone will get to hear your side of the story. Maybe you'll even be able to persuade a jury to let you go free."

It would never happen, but maybe Damian believed in his own superiority to such an extent that he was prepared to believe it. Maybe Paige could persuade him that he needed that kind of public forum so that people could give him the attention he thought he deserved.

The only problem with that was that he'd already made it clear that he was there for one thing and one thing only: to kill her.

"Shut up," Damian said. "You're not the one in charge here. I am. I'm the one with a knife to your partner's face. Which means that I get to tell you what to do."

"Take the shot, Paige," Christopher said, obviously willing to risk everything if it would end this quickly.

Paige knew what the FBI handbook said about situations like this: that it was better to take a shot if one became available, because there was no way of knowing what might or might not drive the hostage taker to kill their captive.

Paige knew all of that in theory, but here, faced with a killer holding Christopher hostage, it was suddenly a lot harder to put into practice. The thought of having to take a life was bad enough; Paige hadn't even done that when a serial killer had been about to kill her mother. The thought of missing and accidentally hurting or even killing Christopher was far worse, though. The prospect of it filled Paige with dread. She couldn't risk it.

"Do it," Christopher said. "Take the shot."

There was another problem, though, even beyond the risks involved.

"I don't have a clean shot," Paige said. If it came to it, she might take a shot if it was there, but she wasn't going to just shoot through Christopher to take down a killer. She wasn't even going to take the risk that she might hit him.

Damian pulled back the knife dramatically, as if he might thrust it home there and then.

"Shut up, both of you! You aren't in control here. *I'm* in control. I decide what happens next."

"You're in control," Paige said, trying to reassure him. She needed to make him feel like he had the power here, because for a narcissist like him, the moment he didn't feel in control he was more likely to lash out. "You decide exactly what happens."

That at least seemed to mollify him enough to stop him from stabbing Christopher there and then.

"You're right," he said. "I do. You're going to do exactly what I say, when I say it, or I'll kill him."

"What do you want me to do?" Paige asked.

"Shut up, I'm trying to think!" He looked both angry and slightly puzzled, as if he hadn't thought about how any of this would go, and hated the fact that he didn't know. He'd come here with a simple plan to kill her, and now that things were going wrong, he probably felt like he wasn't in control anymore.

That was dangerous, because the more out of control Damian felt, the more chance there was of him lashing out blindly.

Paige started to move around Damian and Christopher. She didn't have a shot right now, but maybe if she could create more of an angle, then maybe she would have a chance to take a clean shot at Damian without risking Christopher's life. Paige didn't want to have to do it, but she could feel how this situation was destabilizing, and Paige knew that she couldn't let it go too far without being prepared for it.

Paige realized that, in a sense, both she and Damian were looking for the same thing. They both wanted more control in the situation, and the battle here was over which of them managed to gain it. It was just as lethal a struggle as when they'd been fighting, even though right now neither of them was actively trying to hurt the other.

"Stay there!" Damian said, turning Christopher so that he was still between them. "Do you think I don't know what you're doing? Do you think I haven't been a step ahead of you since all of this began? *Do you?*"

"No, of course not," Paige said, although it was pretty clear to her that Damian was anything but in control of what was happening. That was making the situation more dangerous by the moment.

Paige looked over to Christopher, silently asking him if he was all right. Christopher gave the barest of nods, a tiny movement, but Paige was so used to watching him closely that she made it out easily. He raised an eyebrow slightly, obviously asking Paige if she had a plan.

Paige shook her head very slightly. She didn't have anything yet, but she was working on it. She silently tried to ask him if he had any ideas, and got a maybe in response.

"Ok," Damian said. "I've worked this out. I know how this is going to go. You've insulted my honor, and there's only one penalty for that."

"You want to kill me?" Paige asked. If Damian wanted to try that, then she would welcome it. It would mean him letting go of Christopher. "Then come and stab me the way you stabbed the others."

"What, and have you shoot me the moment I come forward?" Damian demanded. "Do you think I'm stupid? That's what you said to the press, isn't it?"

"No, I don't think you're stupid," Paige said. "I said that to bring you here."

"So you lied about me to the press instead," Damian said. "That isn't any better. You still need to pay."

"So come here and make me pay," Paige said. She put her gun on the floor. "Here, I'll even put my gun down."

It was a terrible risk, because if Damian decided to kill Christopher then, Paige wouldn't have any way to stop him. The problem was, though, that even if Paige had her gun in her hand, it still didn't look like she would have a way to get a clear shot. It didn't do her any good if she couldn't fire without Christopher being killed. She couldn't risk him like that, didn't want to risk losing him, even if he could never truly be hers.

At the very least, she wasn't going to lose her partner. She couldn't. She would take any risk if it provided a chance to save him.

"I'm not falling for that, either," Damian said. "I go for you and your partner shoots me in the back. Maybe I should kill him and then cut you down."

"No!" It was exactly what Paige had been worried about.

Damian made a mocking face. "Oh, so worried for him. What is it? Are you sleeping with him? An uncouth thing like you, I assume that's what you're doing with anyone you can get to."

Paige swallowed at the taunt. Had Damian actually spotted the feelings she had towards Christopher, or was he just so contemptuous of any women who insulted him that he assumed that the only way Paige could be an agent was to sleep her way through the FBI?

"Well, if you don't want me to hurt him, you're going to have to do what I say," Damian said.

Paige could see Christopher's hand starting to inch towards his jacket. She realized that he was trying to get to his gun without Damian noticing. Christopher gave her a pointed look. It was obvious to Paige what he wanted from her: he needed her to distract Damian, and to buy him time.

"All right," Paige said. "I'll do whatever you say."

"Then this is how this is going to go," Damian said. "You're going to do the honorable thing to make up for your insults. You're going to pick up your gun, put it to your head, and kill yourself. If you do that, I'll let your partner here live. If you don't do it, then I'll kill him."

"If you kill him, I'll kill you," Paige replied. She was surprised to find that she meant it. If Damian killed Christopher, then she knew that she wouldn't be trying to bring him in. She would snatch up her gun and fire until Damian was down.

"You can try," Damian said.

That was the problem with the threat: it only worked if Damian truly believed that he would die as a consequence of killing Christopher. He might actually believe that he could stab Christopher, and then get to Paige before she could snatch her gun up again to take him down.

If he was actually prepared to kill Christopher, then he had the advantage.

"Pick up the gun," Damian said.

Paige edged towards it slowly.

"If I do this, what guarantees do I have that you'll let Agent Marriott go?"

She already knew that there *were* no guarantees beyond the word of a killer, but every second that Paige could draw this out was a second in which Christopher could get closer to his service weapon.

"Only my magnanimity, and the fact that *he* hasn't insulted me," Damian said. "Now pick up the gun. Do it, or I'll kill him."

Paige swallowed and lifted the Glock, her horror at having to do it slowing her movements. She watched as she did so for any sign that she might be able to get off a shot, but Damian was still blocking her line of sight using Christopher, so that there was no chance of hitting him without hitting Christopher as well.

"Quicker!" Damian said. "Chamber a round. I want to hear it."

Paige pulled back the slide, as slowly and dramatically as she could. She was grateful for it because it bought another second or two. Christopher's hand was under his jacket now, still moving steadily towards his weapon.

"Now, lift the gun and put it to your head," Damian instructed. "Right to your temple. Do it."

Paige started to lift the weapon, fear starting to rise in her. What if Christopher didn't get to his weapon fast enough? What if Damian put her in a position where she either had to pull the trigger or watch Christopher die. If that happened, which would she do?

Paige didn't know. She really didn't. She didn't want to die, but she also couldn't just stand there and watch Christopher be killed by a madman.

"Put the gun against your head, or he dies," Damian said.

Paige put her gun to her skull feeling the coldness of the metal there. She could feel her heart hammering in her chest at the prospect of having to do this.

"Pull the trigger," Damian instructed, jabbing towards her with the misericord for emphasis. "Do it. Do it now, or I'll-"

That was the moment when Christopher pulled his gun, firing downward in one smooth movement, the sound of the shot filling the parking facility as he shot Damian in the leg.

Damian fell, screaming, flailing with the misericord as if he might still kill both of them. Paige stood over him, gun leveled, and a part of her ached to pull the trigger. After the way he'd just tried to kill Christopher, after the way he'd tried to just kill her…

"Paige, he's down," Christopher said, gently pushing the barrel of her Glock off line. "You're safe."

He stepped forward and kicked the misericord from Damian's hand, sending it spinning away.

"You shot me!" he said, as if he couldn't quite believe that it was possible. "You *shot* me!"

Paige moved in, grabbing his arm, and wrenching him over onto his stomach while she got out her cuffs to restrain him.

"I wasn't lying in the interview," she said. "You're an ordinary, worthless scumbag, Damian Carr. You're also under arrest."

CHAPTER TWENTY SEVEN

Back at the field office, Paige winced as she tried to write up her report for the case. It was hard to do while her hand was bandaged thanks to one of the cuts from Damian's misericord. Paige swore to herself as she typed with the fingers of one hand, setting out what had happened with Damian in the most neutral terms possible.

The suspect took Agent Marriott hostage. I didn't have a clean shot, but was able to keep him talking until Agent Marriott was able to clear his own weapon.

It eluded so much of what had happened back there, leaving out Paige's feelings of terror that Christopher was about to be killed, the feelings towards him that the moment had brought up, which complicated their partnership and made Paige feel faintly guilty every time she looked at him.

He came into the small office that they'd borrowed now, looking pristine and unharmed, save for a couple of small bruises at his throat where Damian's arm had been holding him in place.

"That looks painful," Christopher said, with a glance towards Paige's injured hand.

"It's fine."

"Really? So it wasn't you I heard cursing halfway down the corridor?"

Paige felt herself blush slightly with the embarrassment of that. It wasn't just that Christopher had heard her, but probably everyone else in the field office had too.

"I'm kidding," Christopher said. "I was right outside the door."

Paige breathed a sigh of relief at that, although it still suggested that she'd been too loud.

"Is Damian still in the hospital?" Paige asked.

Christopher nodded. "But it doesn't matter. Between the weapon and the fact that he tried to attack you, we have enough evidence."

"I think he'll talk anyway," Paige said. "He'll confess because he'll want people to know everything he did. He'll see it as the best way of staying important and relevant to people."

"He'll probably write a full biography about it in prison," Christopher said.

It was probably true. A man like Damian Carr would want to continue getting as much attention as he could. He would probably see the whole process of a trial as an affront, but Paige doubted that he would respond to that by going quiet and hiding behind his lawyers. He would be vocal. If anything, the problem was going to be to stop him from talking.

Paige was confident that they were going to get a conviction. Crucially, they'd caught the killer, and no more women in Lexington were going to die at his hand. Paige could only hope that would be enough to provide some solace to the families of Gisele Newbury, Meredith Park, and Peggy Cane.

"We've released Julius Bryant," Christopher said.

"Any problems with him?" Paige asked. She half expected him to sue just because it would raise his profile.

"No, he mostly seems happy that he got lots of information about the interior of an FBI field office. He says he's getting a whole chapter out of it."

Paige guessed that was better than getting sued, at least, although she doubted that Julius Bryant would be very happy once he realized that Damian had been caught and there would be no more chapters for his work.

Paige found herself checking the internet for stories about the case, wondering if the press who had been so harsh about her and Christopher's efforts had relented.

FBI catch Fleur-de-lis Killer!

Lexington killer caught in FBI trap!

It seemed that they had. That was an important lesson to remember: that whatever the press were saying in the middle of a case, the story would shift just as long as they managed to actually solve the case.

"Sauer wants to speak to us," Christopher said.

Instantly, Paige felt a surge of dread. The last time she'd spoken to Agent Sauer, he'd been threatening to take her job away, or reassign her. She couldn't imagine him being as forgiving as the press when it came to everything that had happened in the parking structure.

"It's going to be all right," Christopher said, but even he didn't sound entirely certain about it. Paige realized that he was worried too. Probably he thought that Sauer wouldn't be happy that a suspect had managed to get him into a position where he had a knife to Christopher's throat.

They walked together over to a conference room in the field office, where Agent Sauer's lean features were already up there on a large screen. It was hard to read his expression.

"Agent Sauer," Paige said.

"Agent King, Agent Marriott. So, the news reports are saying that you caught the killer."

"Yes, sir," Christopher said. "Paige's plan to lure him in worked. He tried to kill her, and we were able to apprehend him."

That seemed to bring the faintest note of happiness to Agent Sauer's features.

"I'm glad that you got him. Congratulations, Agents. You've taken a dangerous man off the streets, and with luck, it will mean that the bureau will get some positive press on this too. Lexington PD deciding to ignore you on this one means that we took all the blame when things were going badly, but should also mean that we get the upside of that too."

It was hard for Paige to listen to her boss immediately switching to the optics of all of this, rather than continuing to focus on the fact that they'd just taken down a dangerous criminal, but she guessed that was a part of his job, looking out for the reputation of the department so that they could continue to take down killers. And she could hardly complain when her own instincts had made her check for what the press were saying about her and Christopher in the wake of it all.

"You did well to catch this guy," Agent Sauer said, but the happiness in his expression started to fade a little. "However, we need to talk about exactly what happened out there. You put a plan in place, and called in multiple agents to help secure the area of your hotel. Then the actual arrest took place in a parking garage that was never mentioned in your plans."

He made it sound as if they'd somehow misled him with their plans, rather than Paige and Christopher just being caught up in a dangerous situation that had taken them by surprise.

"With respect, sir," Christopher said. "That situation emerged because the killer ambushed Paige in a location we didn't predict. She could have been killed."

"Yes," Agent Sauer said. "She could, and that's what worries me. Your call on the way the killer would react was good, Agent King, but your assumption that you could control where and when he would react was way off base. It went from a controlled situation to an uncontrolled situation, on the basis of a plan you formed against the judgement of both myself and your partner."

"Sir, I told you," Christopher said. "I supported Paige's plan."

"Which is why you called me about it in the first place?" Sauer asked. "I get that you want to support your partner, but the truth is that this was a dangerous situation that shouldn't have happened."

Paige didn't feel like they could hold back any longer. If she was going to lose her job anyway, then why not? "What was the alternative, sir?"

"Agent King?"

Paige didn't back down. "What was the alternative? If we'd let this go, the killer would still be out there. He might already have murdered another woman by now. Yes, this placed me in danger, and yes, it wasn't in the controlled circumstances that we envisaged, but I'm *paid* to put myself in danger. I'm trained for it, and I'm happy that I was the one he attacked rather than an innocent civilian."

Agent Sauer seemed a little taken aback by that.

"Your job is to catch bad guys, Agent King," he said, in a disapproving tone. "And I don't want my agents putting themselves in danger unnecessarily. You could have been killed, and so could Agent Marriott. I also don't like that you ignored me on this. We *will* talk about this more once you're back in Quantico. But you're right, you caught a killer. Well done. Finish up there and then get back here."

Agent Sauer shut down the video call, leaving Paige and Christopher standing there in the aftermath of the debrief. It took Paige several seconds to realize that she was shaking.

"Paige?" Christopher moved over to her instantly. "Are you all right?"

Paige shook her head. It was as if everything was hitting her at once in that moment. She realized right then just how close she'd come to death. She could still feel the press of the gun against her own skull, still see the knife set against Christopher's skin, forcing her to make an awful choice.

"Paige, you're safe," Christopher said. "It's over. We caught him."

Christopher held her there, a steadying presence. Paige felt like he was a point of stillness, holding her in place, giving her plenty of time to settle. The only problem was just how close he was as he did it. This close, Paige could take in the sweet scent of his aftershave, feel the muscles of his arms against her.

She wanted so much in that moment to just lean in and kiss him. Her eyes met his and seemed to lock there. It seemed as if there was a pull there, one that Paige couldn't resist, didn't *want* to resist, and it seemed to her as if Christopher felt the same way.

They both pulled back in the same moment, and just stood there staring at one another.

Christopher spoke first.

"Paige," Christopher said. "I'm sorry. I don't know what this is, but it can't be anything. I… I'm a married man."

"And I'm not that kind of woman," Paige said. "It was a mistake."

"It's not a mistake either of us can afford to make," Christopher said. "You're a great partner, and an amazing woman. I feel… well, it doesn't *matter* what I feel. What matters is that we need to be able to work together without this getting in the way."

Paige nodded, slightly too quickly. It felt as though they were both rushing to say that everything was fine, everything was normal.

"I know," Paige said. "I want that too. I've been so careful."

"Maybe that's the problem. Maybe we need to stop being careful, because that makes it into this thing that seems inevitable," Christopher said. "We just need to behave normally around one another. We're a good team, and I don't want to lose that."

"Me neither," Paige said. "We work well together."

They were a good team, but that was *all* they could be.

"We need to get back to Quantico," Christopher said. "Agent Sauer will be waiting for us, and…"

Paige understood. Once they got back there, they could take a day or two to get some space from one another. They could focus on work again, and Christopher could get back to his wife.

Maybe it would be good to be back there for Paige, too. It would give her a chance to recover and clear her head. It would give her a chance to focus on the Exsanguination Killer again, too. Maybe once she got home, she would finally be able to find some answers.

EPILOGUE

Paige was back in her apartment, wondering if there was still a chance that she might lose her job in the next few days. Agent Sauer had sounded as though he'd accepted her and Christopher's explanations before, but he'd also said that he wanted to talk to them again once they were back in Quantico.

Paige had only just become an FBI agent; she had no wish to lose that job now. Especially not when it had given her the chance to look deeper into the case that had haunted her since she was fourteen years old: the Exsanguination Killer.

Paige was putting off the moment when she knew she would start working on her carefully crafted file on the killer again, trying to factor in what she knew now about the notes the killer left and the murder weapon. She *knew* that she was putting it off, because she was scared of what she might find. Or rather, what she might *not* find.

Paige knew that her biggest fear was that there wouldn't be anything in the evidence that could help to get her closer to the killer. After all, these were details that the whole of the FBI had been in possession of for years, but they still hadn't managed to find anything based on them.

Would Christopher help her with this if Paige asked? Paige guessed that he might, although after what had almost happened in Lexington, things were still complicated between them. She wanted to be able to treat him like just a partner, but could she really do that if she was asking him for more? For him to go with her into something that wasn't officially their business?

To distract herself from that thought, Paige went down to collect whatever mail she'd missed in the days she'd been in Lexington, walking downstairs to the solid row of metal mailboxes that dominated the wall next to the block's entrance. Paige grabbed the mail without really looking at it, heading back upstairs and setting it down on her couch while she went to get her laptop, and the thick file where she'd pinned newspaper cuttings and handwritten notes. Paige had more notes on her laptop, pulling them up in front of her.

She couldn't put this off any longer; she needed to look over the evidence and see if she could get anything else from it.

She started to work through it, adding in what she knew thanks to Sauer. There was the information about the murder weapon being some kind of scalpel. There was the note, taunting the FBI and the police for their inability to catch the killer. Both provided clues to the kind of person the Exsanguination Killer was: obsessed with control, even up to the moment of death. The way they killed suggested that the control was almost more important than the killing, certainly more important than any violence involved in it. If anything, the killer seemed to avoid excessive, extra violence.

But that didn't get her any closer to the killer's identity. None of it did. That was what was so frustrating about these crimes: the killer was good at leaving no traces, aside from the ones they chose. They killed their sets of three for reasons that only they understood, and then faded away as if they had never been there.

The frustration was intense. Paige set down her laptop, putting her head in her hands as she tried to think. But there was nothing to think *about*, nothing that could get her closer to an answer.

Paige went to open her mail, not knowing what else to do. It turned out to be the usual collection of bills and junk mail, except for one thing.

An envelope sat there with a postmark on it that had come from the St. Just Institute, the high security psychiatric institution where Paige had completed the research for her Ph.D.

That caught Paige by surprise. She hadn't been expecting anything from there, hadn't been back since the night the serial killer Adam Riker had escaped to torment her. The only part left of her life there was that she still communicated with Professor Thornton, her thesis supervisor. It was only a few months, but already it felt like a lifetime ago.

Paige opened the letter, wondering what it could be. The moment she saw the writing there, though, Paige felt like something cold had washed through her blood, all the way to her heart.

Hello Paige,

I saw the news that the Exsanguination Killer has re-emerged. Quite fascinating, in their own way. I'm sure you're sitting there in that apartment of yours, poring over all the details, trying to find some way to get to the murderer who killed your father. And failing, of course. You don't have the information you need.

I do.

All the time you were talking to me and you never asked the one question that matters. I know who the Exsanguination Killer is, Paige.

Come talk to me. Maybe I'll even give you answers.

Adam

Paige found herself breathing faster at that name. Adam Riker had written to her. Paige had thought that he was gone from her life, and he'd *written* to her.

Paige's first instinct was to tear up the letter. Her second was to call the institute to ensure that Adam could never do it again. To make sure that he never contacted her again, and to ignore him.

But Paige couldn't ignore him, not after what he'd just written.

"He's lying," Paige said to herself. "He has to be."

But what if he wasn't? Adam Riker was smart and resourceful to an almost frightening degree. Was it possible that he actually had found out something about the Exsanguination Killer?

Paige knew that if she ignored that possibility, she would always regret it, and that meant exactly one thing:

She had to go to speak with Adam again.

NOW AVAILABLE!

THE GIRL HE CROWNED
(A Paige King FBI Suspense Thriller—Book 5)

Paige King, a Ph.D. in forensic psychology and a new arrival at the FBI's elite BAU unit, has an uncanny ability to enter serial killers' minds—yet nothing has prepared her for what she finds at a series of new crime scenes: a swinging pendulum. What could this serial killer be hinting at? Could he be ticking down the time until the next victim's death?

"A masterpiece of thriller and mystery."
—Books and Movie Reviews, Roberto Mattos (re *Once Gone*)

THE GIRL HE CROWNED is book #5 in a new series by #1 bestselling and critically acclaimed mystery and suspense author Blake Pierce.

A complex psychological crime thriller full of twists and turns and packed with heart-pounding suspense, the PAIGE KING mystery series will make you fall in love with a brilliant new female protagonist and keep you turning pages late into the night. It is a perfect addition for fans of Rachel Caine, Teresa Driscoll and Robert Dugoni.

Book #6 in the series—THE GIRL HE WATCHED—is now also available!

"An edge of your seat thriller in a new series that keeps you turning pages! ...So many twists, turns and red herrings... I can't wait to see what happens next."
—Reader review (*Her Last Wish*)

"A strong, complex story about two FBI agents trying to stop a serial killer. If you want an author to capture your attention and have you guessing, yet trying to put the pieces together, Pierce is your author!"

—Reader review (*Her Last Wish*)

"A typical Blake Pierce twisting, turning, roller coaster ride suspense thriller. Will have you turning the pages to the last sentence of the last chapter!!!"
—Reader review (*City of Prey*)

"Right from the start we have an unusual protagonist that I haven't seen done in this genre before. The action is nonstop... A very atmospheric novel that will keep you turning pages well into the wee hours."
—Reader review (*City of Prey*)

"Everything that I look for in a book... a great plot, interesting characters, and grabs your interest right away. The book moves along at a breakneck pace and stays that way until the end. Now on go I to book two!"
—Reader review (*Girl, Alone*)

"Exciting, heart pounding, edge of your seat book... a must read for mystery and suspense readers!"
—Reader review (*Girl, Alone*)

Blake Pierce

Blake Pierce is the USA Today bestselling author of the RILEY PAGE mystery series, which includes seventeen books. Blake Pierce is also the author of the MACKENZIE WHITE mystery series, comprising fourteen books; of the AVERY BLACK mystery series, comprising six books; of the KERI LOCKE mystery series, comprising five books; of the MAKING OF RILEY PAIGE mystery series, comprising six books; of the KATE WISE mystery series, comprising seven books; of the CHLOE FINE psychological suspense mystery, comprising six books; of the JESSE HUNT psychological suspense thriller series, comprising twenty-four books; of the AU PAIR psychological suspense thriller series, comprising three books; of the ZOE PRIME mystery series, comprising six books; of the ADELE SHARP mystery series, comprising sixteen books, of the EUROPEAN VOYAGE cozy mystery series, comprising four books; of the new LAURA FROST FBI suspense thriller, comprising nine books (and counting); of the new ELLA DARK FBI suspense thriller, comprising eleven books (and counting); of the A YEAR IN EUROPE cozy mystery series, comprising nine books, of the AVA GOLD mystery series, comprising six books (and counting); of the RACHEL GIFT mystery series, comprising six books (and counting); of the VALERIE LAW mystery series, comprising nine books (and counting); of the PAIGE KING mystery series, comprising six books (and counting); of the MAY MOORE mystery series, comprising nine books (and counting); of the CORA SHIELDS mystery series, comprising three books (and counting); and of the NICKY LYONS mystery series, comprising three books (and counting).

An avid reader and lifelong fan of the mystery and thriller genres, Blake loves to hear from you, so please feel free to visit www.blakepierceauthor.com to learn more and stay in touch.

BOOKS BY BLAKE PIERCE

NICKY LYONS MYSTERY SERIES
ALL MINE (Book #1)
ALL HIS (Book #2)
ALL HE SEES (Book #3)

CORA SHIELDS MYSTERY SERIES
UNDONE (Book #1)
UNWANTED (Book #2)
UNHINGED (Book #3)

MAY MOORE SUSPENSE THRILLER
NEVER RUN (Book #1)
NEVER TELL (Book #2)
NEVER LIVE (Book #3)
NEVER HIDE (Book #4)
NEVER FORGIVE (Book #5)
NEVER AGAIN (Book #6)
NEVER LOOK BACK (Book #7)
NEVER FORGET (Book #8)
NEVER LET GO (Book #9)

PAIGE KING MYSTERY SERIES
THE GIRL HE PINED (Book #1)
THE GIRL HE CHOSE (Book #2)
THE GIRL HE TOOK (Book #3)
THE GIRL HE WISHED (Book #4)
THE GIRL HE CROWNED (Book #5)
THE GIRL HE WATCHED (Book #6)

VALERIE LAW MYSTERY SERIES
NO MERCY (Book #1)
NO PITY (Book #2)
NO FEAR (Book #3)
NO SLEEP (Book #4)

NO QUARTER (Book #5)
NO CHANCE (Book #6)
NO REFUGE (Book #7)
NO GRACE (Book #8)
NO ESCAPE (Book #9)

RACHEL GIFT MYSTERY SERIES
HER LAST WISH (Book #1)
HER LAST CHANCE (Book #2)
HER LAST HOPE (Book #3)
HER LAST FEAR (Book #4)
HER LAST CHOICE (Book #5)
HER LAST BREATH (Book #6)
HER LAST MISTAKE (Book #7)
HER LAST DESIRE (Book #8)

AVA GOLD MYSTERY SERIES
CITY OF PREY (Book #1)
CITY OF FEAR (Book #2)
CITY OF BONES (Book #3)
CITY OF GHOSTS (Book #4)
CITY OF DEATH (Book #5)
CITY OF VICE (Book #6)

A YEAR IN EUROPE
A MURDER IN PARIS (Book #1)
DEATH IN FLORENCE (Book #2)
VENGEANCE IN VIENNA (Book #3)
A FATALITY IN SPAIN (Book #4)

ELLA DARK FBI SUSPENSE THRILLER
GIRL, ALONE (Book #1)
GIRL, TAKEN (Book #2)
GIRL, HUNTED (Book #3)
GIRL, SILENCED (Book #4)
GIRL, VANISHED (Book 5)
GIRL ERASED (Book #6)
GIRL, FORSAKEN (Book #7)
GIRL, TRAPPED (Book #8)

GIRL, EXPENDABLE (Book #9)
GIRL, ESCAPED (Book #10)
GIRL, HIS (Book #11)

LAURA FROST FBI SUSPENSE THRILLER
ALREADY GONE (Book #1)
ALREADY SEEN (Book #2)
ALREADY TRAPPED (Book #3)
ALREADY MISSING (Book #4)
ALREADY DEAD (Book #5)
ALREADY TAKEN (Book #6)
ALREADY CHOSEN (Book #7)
ALREADY LOST (Book #8)
ALREADY HIS (Book #9)

EUROPEAN VOYAGE COZY MYSTERY SERIES
MURDER (AND BAKLAVA) (Book #1)
DEATH (AND APPLE STRUDEL) (Book #2)
CRIME (AND LAGER) (Book #3)
MISFORTUNE (AND GOUDA) (Book #4)
CALAMITY (AND A DANISH) (Book #5)
MAYHEM (AND HERRING) (Book #6)

ADELE SHARP MYSTERY SERIES
LEFT TO DIE (Book #1)
LEFT TO RUN (Book #2)
LEFT TO HIDE (Book #3)
LEFT TO KILL (Book #4)
LEFT TO MURDER (Book #5)
LEFT TO ENVY (Book #6)
LEFT TO LAPSE (Book #7)
LEFT TO VANISH (Book #8)
LEFT TO HUNT (Book #9)
LEFT TO FEAR (Book #10)
LEFT TO PREY (Book #11)
LEFT TO LURE (Book #12)
LEFT TO CRAVE (Book #13)
LEFT TO LOATHE (Book #14)
LEFT TO HARM (Book #15)